STANDALONE

The Sins That Bind Us

Two Week Turnaround

His Private Collection

beautiful *forever*

GENEVA LEE

beautiful *forever*

GENEVA LEE

IVY ESTATE

To Josh,
who saw it coming

LATER

At Belle Mère Prep, some kids come back to school after a summer in Europe. Others return with a few new notches on their Restoration Hardware bedposts. So? I'm coming back with a security detail.

They can stare at me in the hallways. Who can blame them? The fact is that I spent most of my summer as a lead suspect in a murder case. My classmates gawk as I take a seat. No doubt they're trying to spot a baby bump. It's the only way this could get any better for them.

Thanks a lot, TMZ.

But while they stare, I can only think of those people that aren't here this morning to start their senior year. I feel their absences as ominously as an unexplained shadow in an empty room. Some are long gone. One didn't see the end of the summer.

Living or dead, they're just ghosts now.

Chances are choices. Or something like that. For instance, take opening a door to find someone completely unexpected on the other side. To shut the door or feign surprise. A kind person might give the guilty party across from them a gracious out. But no one has ever accused me of being nice. Not to Monroe West, anyway.

"Monroe." I greet her by the name I know as she flies into the room. Then I remember myself. "I mean, May. I see you've landed yourself your dream job."

May West. There's a certain poetry to it. I wonder if she was being clever or if she unintentionally chose such a famous alias. Her usually stick-straight hair waves into soft curls over her shoulders and she's wearing enough eyeshadow to make a porn star blush. She's gone from looking like an entitled seventeen year-old Houser to passing for a hard-used twenty-five-year-old showgirl. If we weren't standing so closely I might not have recognized her as my fellow classmate, boyfriend's sister, and, dare I add, psychotic bitch? We'd made some minor progress on that front of late but something tells me this less-than-chance encounter would put us right back at square one.

Monroe tugs up the silver, sequined tube masquerading as a dress and glares at me. I have to give her credit. The momentary flash of fear that I'd spotted when I opened the door is hidden behind a mask of annoyance. Despite the audacious dress, she doesn't look out of place in the five-star hotel room. Then again every aspect of the West Casino hotel room from the slight sheen in the wall-paper to the overstocked mini bar screams style over substance. Apparently, it's a trait Nathaniel West's hotels shared with his own family.

"How much?" she asks through gritted teeth.

"I thought I was the one who paid you." I lean against the hotel door, closing it behind us. As soon as the lock clicks her eyes narrow.

"I'm not interested in your little jokes," she hisses. "Tell me how much you need to keep quiet."

I blow a stream of air between my lips. "A pony. The lost city of Atlantis. Maybe a trip to see the Wizard."

I don't suffer from any misconceptions. If the situation were reversed, the Wicked Bitch of the West, aka my darling Monroe, wouldn't hesitate to blast the news of my fall from virtue to every student at Belle Mère Prep. But I'm not here for that. I've come to this hotel room for one reason: The Dealer.

A few days ago, a mysterious new photo had shown up

on The Dealer's feed. I hadn't expected it to lead me to an escort agency. When I realized where I was I gambled and pretended to be interested in a job. The ploy worked, granting me enough time to schedule an appointment with May: the only clue The Dealer had attached to his post.

But why lead me here? What did Monroe's extracurricular activities have to do with the night that Nathaniel West died? I thought the purpose of the Instagram account was to expose the killer. I'm not so certain anymore. Unless The Dealer's plan is simply to disgrace each of us as thoroughly as possible.

Monroe steps closer to me, jabbing a finger in my chest. "How did you even find out?"

I sidle away toward the minibar. Grabbing two tiny bottles of West Tennessee Whiskey, I toss her one. She can play it cool but I know she needs liquid courage as much as I do.

She rolls her eyes when she reads the label and sashays over. "I prefer gin."

"Doesn't your family own West Tennessee Whiskey?" I ask as I screw off the cap and down mine in a single gulp. It blazes down my throat, lighting a fire in my stomach.

"Yes, but my family owns everything." There's a brittle edge in her words but she swallows it down along with her shot of whiskey. Then she digs out another mini bottle of Beefeater.

"What are you doing?" I ask her and suddenly this isn't an interrogation. I'm not trying to pry information out of her. Instead I find myself wanting to shake her. I may have no love for Monroe West, but I know what this would do to her family. I like her mother, but I was in love with her brother. With everything the two of them have been through this year, this might destroy the fragile threads holding their family together.

"Why would you care?"

That's a cry for help if I've ever heard one. "Because The Dealer sent me here, which means that anyone else who's following his posts could have opened that door."

It's only a matter of time before the police and FBI catch on to the account. That will be bad enough. Right now, only a handful of people are following the mysterious feed, and each of them has good reason to want to know the identity of our friendly neighborhood stalker. The Dealer hasn't been posting our proudest moments so no one has started sharing the pictures—yet.

"What does he have on you?" she asks, her eyes flash as if something important has finally occurred to her.

So much for hoping that Monroe is as smart as she looks. I'd had my suspicions that the blonde, air-head heiress act was for show, now I know it is. If I'm following The Dealer closely enough to wind up here it's not out of curiosity.

I shrug. Two blondes can play dumb.

"Maybe the proof that Mackey is looking for." She pours another glass, but she doesn't down it this time. Sipping thoughtfully, she watches me for a sign that she's right.

"Sorry to disappoint you, but he's got nothing." None

of the photos on the feed seemed directed at me, but plenty of them focused on people around me. Of course, the company I keep has as good as convicted me in the eyes of the FBI. "I know what it will take for me to keep quiet."

"Yes?" she snaps. For a second I almost swear her eyes flash a demonic red, but that's probably just me.

"The truth." If Monroe expects me to keep quiet about this discovery, then I'm going to need to know why she's doing it in the first place.

"The truth is in short supply these days." She drops into a chair and stares out the window at the sparkling city lights. Even in the daylight, Vegas flashes its best smile, calling tourists to come hither with promises of good luck and good fortune. Monroe's gaze grows distant as if she's as lost to this city as anyone else.

"Why?" I continue. "You have everything. Why throw it away?"

"You think I'm throwing it away?" Her head whips around so she can glare directly at me. "Do you know what Vegas is? A place for dreamers. It's easy to lose your way here. Ask your daddy."

"Ask yours," I counter coldly.

She flinches but shrugs it off with a hollow laugh. Flipping her hair over her shoulder, she goes on. "You can either lose yourself or you can make yourself."

I'm pretty certain that Monroe West already has it made, but I keep the thought to myself. If I keep provoking her, I'll never get my answer.

"My father made himself into a mogul. Everyone

expects me to spend the rest of my life in the spa or shopping. I don't have to work." Her eyes flicker over to check if I'm listening. I nod for her to continue. "But I don't want to be another parasitic heiress. God knows the world has enough of those."

"You want to be a hooker instead?" The question slips out, and I clamp my mouth shut. When you operate at my level of sarcasm, it's hard to contain it.

"I'm not a hooker," she says with a withering look.

"Escort," I correct myself, tacking on a "sorry."

"My father made his fortune on gamblers. He made money on money. Jameson gets to take over that empire. No work. No hardship. It's just his."

"I doubt he sees it that way." Defensiveness flares in my chest at the mention of my boyfriend.

"Of course not. He, like most men, has the luxury of being able to complain about his circumstances while still taking advantage of them." She wags her finger at the space between us. "We don't."

Now I'm in the same class as Monroe? Will wonders never cease? Although, I don't expect that our two-girl Breakfast Club is going to meet again after we leave this room.

"There's plenty of money in Vegas. It's almost an insult to make money on money."

"So you're going to make money off sex?" I guess.

"I'm going to build my empire on sex," she corrects me. "The youngest madam in Vegas history. I've learned the trade from some of the best, and let's face it, I'm well-educated."

I thought back to English class. I suppose you don't need a spectacular grasp of the classics to run an escort agency.

"I won't have any competition." She leaves the last statement lingering in the air as bait.

I bite. "And why is that?"

"Because they'll all be terrified that I'll reveal that they employed me while I was underage. Instead I get to play the part of business savant," she concludes.

She already has the part of idiot down, I think.

Monroe studies me for a moment. No doubt wondering what I think of her now. "If things don't work out with Jameson, I might have a job for you."

"I don't think we should be in business together," I say dryly. Having Monroe as my high school enemy and my pimp is a bit much to swallow.

"You know where to find me," she says, unfazed. "If you'll excuse me, I have better things to do with my day and you must have...something to do with yours."

Like your brother.

When she leaves, I settle onto the bed and stare at the ceiling above. Various shapes emerge from the spackle like pieces of a mysterious puzzle. There was one question I didn't think to ask Monroe: why would The Dealer want to out her? I'm beginning to question if my eyes were playing tricks on me before. I check my phone for a response but there is none. When I open Instagram, the photo is gone.

It looks like The Dealer got my message and made a move after all. It should be a victory but instead it feels like I've painted a big target on my back.

MY SANDALS CLICK across the marble floor of the West Resort lobby. Slot machines ring out in the distance and even here I can taste the stale cigarette smoke from the casino floor. It's the same as every hotel and casino in this town. Arguably a little nicer than most. So why is it the current epicenter for crime in a city that's no stranger to vice?

This is where the mystery began for me. Is this where it started for a murderer as well? It's hard to believe that months have passed since the deadly party that dragged me into this world. I hadn't even wanted to go, but my best friend, Josie, who desperately wants to be in with the cool crowd, shanghaied me into attending Monroe West's end-of-the-year party. It was supposed to be a celebration of the last day of our junior year—one that I wasn't invited to attend.

We crashed, and I'd be lying if I said I didn't enjoy the look on Monroe's face when she caught me. The two of us had never gotten along, especially after Monroe screwed my boyfriend in front of half of our freshman class. It had been war between the two of us ever since, and trespassing on her party was a declaration of battle. I'd wanted to leave after the confrontation, but instead of tracking down Josie, I met someone. He was a stranger, but something about him put me at ease. We'd spent the night together. Not in the Biblical sense but pretty damn close. The next morning, he was gone.

As if waking up alone in my best enemy's house wasn't bad enough, I'd been forced to hitch a ride with my ex-boyfriend, Jonas, and his smarmy best friend, Hugo. I thought that was the end to a night I'd rather forget—until news broke out that Nathaniel West had been murdered.

The prime suspects? Everyone who'd been at his daughter's party. I might have gotten away with a simple questioning until I found out that the guy I'd shacked up with that night was Jameson West—the heir to the West fortune and the victim's son. Obviously, I have questionable taste in men. Not as strange as my best friend Josie's penchant for older men—a vice that sent her to some dude's hotel room and left me needing an alibi.

Jameson was everyone's number one suspect, even mine. Especially after he started showing up wherever I was. Despite his stalker tendencies, I decided to find out for myself. I never expected to fall in love with him.

I know he's innocent, but that hasn't removed either of us from suspicion in the eyes of the FBI. So, when a mysterious Instagram account ran by someone known only as The Dealer started posting incriminating photos of Belle Mère Prep's most-likely-to-be-a-murderer list, I took it upon myself to investigate. I need to clear our names, and I can only do that if I figure out who killed Nathaniel West.

But as of this afternoon something weighs more heavily on my mind. Thanks to the FBI's resident pain in the ass, Agent Mackey, I have to worry if I can be in love with Jameson. I already learned that my sister was another man's child, a fact my parents kept from me even after her death, but I never considered that I might be as well. If Mackey isn't lying, and I think it's entrapment or some other Law and Order no-go if she is, then I have more than one mystery to solve. Only time will tell if Nancy Drew and the Mystery of the Baby Daddy, starring yours truly, will have a happy ending.

It's not true. I am not Nathaniel West's daughter.

I repeat the thought in my head like a new-age manifestation. I have to believe it, because if I don't the pit widening in my stomach will swallow me whole.

The question plagues me as I reach the revolving door, but before I can step inside, a hand closes over my shoulder and spins me around. With my mind lost in thoughts of felonies, I shriek. The sound is smothered by Jameson West's lips.

Jerking away, I try to ignore the urge to melt into him.

In his suit, he looks older than he really is. There's even a faint trace of stubble peppering his jaw. I run my fingers over it without thinking and he sighs. Rubbing it with his hand, he shakes his head. "I shaved this morning, Duchess."

"It makes you look powerful."

His eyebrow curves up like a question mark. "It makes me look old."

After his father's unexpected death, Jameson stepped up to run the family business. Given that the last argument he'd had with his father was about him dropping out of college, he hadn't planned to be running a Fortune 500 company. The new responsibilities might be aging him, and sharing any info I've learned today won't help.

I look for the truth in his face, but all I find is the strong set of his jawline and unreadable expression in his silver eyes. His unruly, coppery hair is tamed into submission. Today he's playing the part of the businessman. Aloof. Untouchable. Calculating. And I'm the one he's analyzing. I shrink away from him.

"What's wrong?" The suspicion in his voice only sharpens my edginess.

"Nothing," I lie too quickly to be believable. "You surprised me."

"I was about to say the same thing," he says slowly. "Are you hear to see me?"

"Why would I be here to see you?" I really need some verbal Pepto-Bismol right now to stop all the paranoia from spewing out of me.

"Because I work here, Duchess. I was overseeing the security updates." He pauses to give me a chance to connect the dots but my brain has gone haywire. "I sent you a text."

"My phone's acting strangely." Apparently, the dishonesty is going to give the paranoia a run for its money.

"I have a few minutes. Why don't I give you the private tour of the business offices?"

I sidestep him when he reaches for me. Hurt flashes over his features, but he smiles tightly. "I'm sorry. Josie's sick and I have to run and if we get started..."

He allows me to bow out, gracelessly I might add, without further comment, but before the revolving door seals behind me, he calls out one final question, "Why were you here?"

I step out on the other side, and we stare at each other through the glass. I could go back inside and explain, but facing him is painful enough. Maybe this was always our destiny: to see each other but never touch.

Standing outside Josie's cracker box house, I can't help but see it for the tiny two-bedroom block that it is. I'd been by earlier today in an attempt to make amends, and it hadn't struck me then, but with my world topsy-turvy, I guess I'm seeing everything in a new light. I've spent the last few months bouncing between billionaires like a bad episode of MTV's Cribs, but being here, now, all that matters is that it feels like I'm finally home. If I'm an impostor in my own life, then it's time to take a step back and return to the people who know and love me.

Even with this new-found resolve, I knock tentatively at the door. Marion, Josie's mother, opens it with a surprised look on her face.

"Since when did you knock?" she asks. And there it is: I am home. This is where I belong, and who I belong with. She's fresh faced with her hair pulled back in a tight knot.

It takes a minute for me to remember that it's Friday night. "Sorry honey, but I'm on my way out. I have to get to the dressing rooms in 30 minutes."

Such is the life of a Las Vegas showgirl on the weekend. She'll spend the next couple of days fending off the advances of overly confident businessmen, and the scummy men in town for bachelor parties. They'll pop in and out of Vegas, leaving nothing but a forgettable trail of debt following their two-night stint.

"I actually came to see Josie," I tell her.

Her eyebrows quirk together. "She's sick, and you know how she is when she's sick."

"I do know how my best friend acts when she's sick."

Hospitals were invented for people like Josie Deckard who could turn every cough into consumption. Since I've known her, she's had a habit of quarantining herself at the first sign of a sniffle. Back then, I was allowed to leave offerings of Disney Channel movies at her door, but never permitted to enter. Even Marion had to talk her way inside. But today is a different story, and her hypochondria will have to take a backseat to me pulling the best friend card.

I hesitate. If I tell Marion my sad story, she'll offer me the couch, which is already mine. But this isn't a decision I can leave up to her. Not with things so weird between Josie and I.

"I'll risk it," I decide out loud. No matter how good it feels to be here, I'll need Josie's blessing if I'm going to reclaim my second home.

Marion kisses me on the cheek and the familiar token of affection eases some of my anxiety. Her skin brushes mine. It's soft and warm, like a mother's cheek is supposed to be. I've based that belief entirely on the maternal surrogacy she's shown me over the years. My own mother favors more of a European air kiss with both strangers and her progeny. The stark contrast between Josie's mom and mine has never felt more evident than at this moment. "Lock the door behind me."

I nod as a lump forms in my throat. This is where I should have been this summer, watching Netflix between shifts at Pawnography, my Dad's shop, planning out every second of my upcoming senior year at Bell-Mère Prep, and keeping Josie and her love life in check. Instead, I'd found myself cast without warning into the role of bad girl socialite. It's time to shed that costume and come back to reality.

Turning the bolt on the front door, I take a deep breath and march down the short hallway to Josie's room. I don't bother to be timid with my knock. Dead silence greets me and after an eternity, a muffled, "Go away."

This is going about as well as I expected.

Trying the knob, I'm not surprised that it's locked, but since this house was built in the 70s, like so much of Vegas, all that stands between me and my reckoning with my best friend is a bobby pin. Slipping one out of my hair, I poke at the tiny hole next to the knob until I hit pay dirt. Home builders must have thought they were doing parents a favor. Give kids the illusion of autonomy by providing a lock on the door that a one cent piece of metal can open.

"Ready or not," I mutter to myself and throw open the door. Josie's buried under her covers, a pillow over her head. Instantly, she sits bolt upright, her cotton fortress crumbling around her as she stares at me.

"I'm not feeling good," she snaps.

I shrug.

"The world is in a state of economic crisis, a reality star is running for president, and we're stuck in a town that still believes second hand smoke is harmless. Nobody's feeling good," I retort. My hands find my hips and I plant them there, ready for whatever she throws at me first, but my defensive posture does nothing to help me when she throws herself backward on the bed.

It takes a second for me to gauge the actual situation in the room. Not much has changed. Neat piles of discarded clothes litter the perimeter. Stacks of notebooks and magazines wait on the desk. She hasn't redecorated or remodeled or turned it into a craft room. Everything is as it should be, but by the time I take my second look around I see a few things that are off. The clothing piles are bigger than they should be. The magazines on her desk are untouched, having been left unread for an entire summer meant to be spent poolside. And most disconcerting, the television isn't on. Everyone from infancy to the infirm knows that the only modern perk of illness is Netflix.

"You aren't sick," I accuse her. "You're hiding. We

might as well get straight to the point. Did you run off when I showed up today?"

It's not like Josie to turn tail and hide from a situation.

"Someone has a pretty high opinion of herself. I guess that's naturally what happens when you're dating a West." She makes the name sound like a curse word, and I'd be lying if I said my hackles didn't rise at the provocation. I circle her bed looking for clues.

"Yep, they initiated me into the secret society of the Housers," I say, imbuing my words with the proper amount of disgust. Neither of us have ever been Housers. That accolade is reserved for Belle Mère's elite, the children of Las Vegas's upper, upper crust. They run the show while the rest of us hope for a spot in the audience. "My shit no longer stinks and I know their special handshake."

She only glares so I continue my analysis.

"Oh my God, would you stop," she finally says. "You're right. I'm not dying, vulture, so if you're waiting to consume my dead body, you can fly off somewhere else."

"Cute, but that's not why I'm here. I have a favor to ask you."

"This is how you ask for a favor?"

Okay, so she might have a point. One of the few pieces of good advice my mother ever gave me was that you catch more flies with honey. I've never been very good at utilizing that strategy, probably since my mother never bothered to model the behavior herself. Plus, Josie and I are past the candy-coated platitudes of false friendship. She's right though. We need to fix this before I can come home again. So naturally, I start by attacking her. "What's going on with you Josie? You've been acting strangely for weeks. Now you're hiding in bed pretending to be sick? Not just from me, but from your mom as well."

There's a silence that stretches the length of the bible, and then she slowly sits up. Now that she's not glaring at me, I can see that her eyes are red-rimmed and bloodshot. Her lip trembles a little. Josie Deckard has been crying. The idea of teenage girl sobbing into her pillow might not seem like an anomaly, but my best friend doesn't fit that description. She never has.

"Where have you been?" she asks me quietly.

It's not as simple a question as it appears to be, and it doesn't deserve a curt response or a cutesy answer. Instead, I lay it all on the line for her. "Under investigation for murder, falling in love, wrecking my entire family, doing incredibly stupid shit and realizing it's been for nothing."

But that's only the beginning, and we both know it. Sitting down on the edge of her bed, I fill her in on all of the details. I know I'm leaving things out, probably important things, but the gist is there. When I'm finished, a huge burden lifts off my shoulders. I've forgotten how hard it is to keep secrets. Even having one person to trust them with lifts the load off my back.

"What about you," I ask her. "I'm not the only one who's been unavailable this summer."

Josie and I were often separated over the last few years during school break. I'd be shipped off to Palm Springs to visit with my mother or be stuck working at my dad's pawn shop. Josie would be stuck at home or taking whatever job she could find to supplement her non-existent allowance. But we called. And later we texted and Facetimed. We made time for sleep-overs and lunch dates and the occasional petty shoplifting. This summer, we have barely sent an emoji to each other.

Josie doesn't respond to my question. Instead, she gets out of bed. It takes a long time, as if she's ordering her limbs to move and willing her body to take each step. Opening her desk drawer, she rifles around for a few minutes until she pulls the false bottom up. We'd concocted that little secret spot to stash contraband over the years. Contraband being a pack of cigarettes when we were going through our we're older than we look phase. A bit of booze. Maybe some condoms. The kind of stuff every parent knows their kid is hiding, but we still bother to hide anyway.

Nothing prepares me for what she pulls out of that drawer though. Having little to no experience with the topic, I stare at the black and white photo for far too long. The paper is flimsy. The image is warped, but I can read.

I can read her name in the corner. I can decipher that the numbers mean weeks and days. Try as I might, the white noise photo in the center doesn't make sense.

"Is this..." I trail away, swallowing the words. If I don't say them, they won't be true.

"An ultrasound," she says. Her voice detaches from her body as she continues on in an all business tone. "The clinic I went to makes you have one before you can make any decisions, even if you already made your decision. Probably some politician's idea of punishment."

She continues on, as if she can replace the tension in the air with her tirades.

"Oh my God," I breath, basically ignoring her. "Did you ... Are you ..."

"I am," she admits.

"Why?" The question bursts out of me. Everything is starting to make sense: her distance and irritability. But there's no relief in this revelation. Rather it feels like I'm waking from a nightmare to discover I wasn't asleep.

She snatches the picture away and shoves it back in the drawer, as if hiding it is in any way dealing with the situation. "All that debate about it and no one tells you how expensive it is to get it done. I've been saving all summer. It's still not enough and ..." she doesn't finish the sentence, but she doesn't have to. The thought of actually going through with it is scary and I'm not even the one who has to do it.

"I can help." It's not an offer because she's taking my help, whether she wants it or not. "I would've helped. Why didn't you tell me?"

"It's complicated."

"Does the father know?"

"He's not in the picture," she says, her nostrils flaring in defiance.

I decide not to press the issue. When she's ready to share more, she will.

"All those years of her being so paranoid," she says

absently, "and I've gone and done the one thing that will break my mom's heart."

"You don't have to tell her," I whisper.

She blinks as if remembering that I'm there and then stares at me. "Em, I can't do this alone."

"You won't have to," I promise.

3

We spend the next few days ignoring our situations in favor of binge-watching as much bad TV as we can stomach. Now that we've spilled our guts it's easier to just sit and digest in each other's presence than to continue strategizing our next moves. I need a break. A break from the investigating, from the suspicion, from watching over my shoulder. I can't even imagine how badly Josie needs a break. I do my best not to stare at her when reality invades my conscious mind over the on-screen action trying to drown it out.

She looks the same. That may be because she hasn't changed her pajama pants in like three days, but really, looking at her you wouldn't even know. Shouldn't there be some type of clue? Is this how getting knocked up works? If so, couldn't we all be knocked up all the time and not know it?

"Stop staring at me," she finally mutters one afternoon. "It's not going to burst out of my abdomen and do a song and dance."

"Sorry," I say sheepishly. "It's just so weird."

She groans, shaking her head as she flips through the Recently Addeds.

"You know what's weird? The fact that you have a security detail parked across the street from my house."

Okay, I can grant her that.

"Let's go back to being 12," I suggest, "when our biggest problem was hoping we could finally get our periods."

As soon as it's out of my mouth, I wish I could take it back, but she just gives a hollow laugh.

"Yeah. I actually kind of feel like I'm hoping to get my period all the time at the moment."

"And the award for shitty friend of the year goes to"— I clutch my chest dramatically—"me. I'd like to thank my mother, who taught me everything I know, my father, who also contributed, and generally just being surrounded by the worst possible role models a girl can have."

Josie's false laughter turns into bemused giggles. "What award do I win? Most likely to become her mother?"

I wince, then nearly jump out of my skin when Josie's mother actually opens the door. If there was an award for appearing innocent, neither of us would be winning it at the moment.

"Em, your mom called me." She stares me down.

I kind of expected that. "I might have blocked her phone number."

Marion pinches the bridge of her nose, sighing heavily and forming the perfect image of the maternal archetype at the same time. "You can't block your mother."

"Funny, my iPhone says I can." I tack on a smile as if to indicate I'm joking, even though we both know I'm not.

"She says that she really needs to talk to you." Marion bypasses the passive-aggressiveness and goes straight for the kill. "I can't have you staying here if your mother doesn't think it's okay."

"My mother wouldn't care if I was living under a bridge," I grumble, but I take out my phone and pull up her number. "I'll call her."

Marion disappears with a look of triumph and Josie bumps her shoulder against mine.

"You want a minute?"

"Nah." I'd already told her everything that had happened. What I'd discovered about Becca, how Hans had tried to corner me. She'd gotten the blow by blow. Whatever mitigating factors my mother wants to add to the drama I won't be keeping from her either.

Mom answers on the first ring.

"Emma," she says breathlessly, as if she's been pacing while waiting for my call.

"Vivian," I respond coolly. She doesn't bother to correct me, even though she hates that I call her by her first name. More than ever, I need that detachment and whatever small sense of self-confidence it grants me.

"We need to talk."

We've needed to talk for the last eight years, but I'm glad she's finally getting the memo.

"I'm not coming to Palm Springs," I say.

Mom isn't the type to have serious conversations over the phone. She believes in tearing someone down to their face, the good old-fashioned way.

"You don't have to," she assures me. "I'm here in Las Vegas."

"What restaurant?" I ask.

"I think it's better if I come to you."

It's taken a lot of years for me to build up enough scar tissue where my mom is concerned that her barbs and dismissals don't hurt me anymore, but apparently, she can still catch me off guard.

"I'm staying at Josie's," I tell her in broken fragments while I try to piece together what could be so terrible that she would deign to leave her five-star life and slum it in the burbs.

"I'll come over this evening," my mom says. "Should I bring McDonald's?"

"Yeah mom, get me a Happy Meal," I say flatly. We hang up and I wonder if she's experiencing some type of medical incident that's caused a temporary bought of amnesia. Maybe she hit her head and thinks I'm nine years-old and that I've been at Josie's for an extended sleepover.

"What was that about?" Josie asks as soon as I'm off the phone.

I give her a look that says way more than what comes out of my mouth next. "Guess who's coming to dinner?"

4

That night my mother actually brings me a Happy Meal.

"I can't remember if you still hate ketchup," she says as she hands the box to me at the door.

"I've made peace with tomatoes," I reassure her as I try to concentrate on the carefully proportioned glut of calories that she's brought me. Who decided apple slices were fast food? But I can't distract myself from the fact that for the first time, in a very long time, it's my mother standing at the door. Not Vivian von Essen.

Her perfectly manicured nails are chewed down to the quick, and she twists her fingers nervously. She's wearing a simple wrap dress instead of a tailored suit and although her hair is done, it hangs flatly over her shoulders. Somehow she's become the before shot in a shampoo commercial.

This is the woman I grew up with—harried, nervous.

My dad's gambling problems made it impossible for his business ventures to succeed. I'd watched her dreams slip away for years, until this was what she looked like. She'd turned herself around then and left behind anyone who might have dragged her back to this state. I'm not sure what it means that she's here now.

Josie tip-toes down the hall to greet her. "Hi Mrs. Von-"

My mother holds up a hand to stop her. "Mrs...um, I mean Vivian is perfectly acceptable, Josie."

Perfectly acceptable. Well, it's good to know that the rod that maintains her stiff formality is still in place.

Josie glances at me worriedly. I'm not imagining that she looks like hell.

"I'll leave you two to talk." With that she disappears.

Mom and I stare at each other. Usually we meet on neutral ground. When she's in Vegas, mom doesn't come to dad's house. We meet for brunches or afternoon tea. Occasionally, she convinces me to go shopping, and while the Deckard's house isn't home to either of us, it's far from neutral.

That means that in my mother's eyes, it's up to me to play the hostess.

"Uh, why don't we sit down and eat," I finally manage. That's about the time I realize she's holding another Happy Meal. Apparently, mom also wants to pretend she's a kid again. I guess adulting doesn't get any easier. She catches me staring at the bag.

"I brought one for Josie," she explains.

"I'll give it to her," I say, seizing the opportunity to run away for a minute.

Josie holds up the sign of the cross when I enter her bedroom.

"I brought you food." I toss the happy meal on her bed like a sacrificial offering.

"I'm still not bailing you out of this."

"Please do not make me talk to her alone," I beg.

"Un-uh."

"I'm revoking your friendship card," I tell her.

"I think I can find someone else to French braid my hair," she teases.

I shut the door a little too hard behind me.

"Josie's been battling the flu," I say as a means to explain why she's hiding out.

"Oh, that's too bad," mom says absently. "It's probably best that we talk alone anyway."

"Aren't you going to eat?" I ask her.

"I wasn't hungry."

That makes two of us. Later, I'm going to regret not eating these French fries, but right now I know I couldn't force them down. Not when my mouth is so dry, it feels like someone shoved half a package of cotton balls in it.

"You look well," she says at the same time I blurt out, "You look like hell."

"Don't say hell," she admonishes me.

"There's no such thing as hell, mom." I've been making the argument since I first dropped the h-bomb to her.

"There is. It's where sinners and unbaptized babies go."

"When did you go Roman Catholic on me?" I ask. She's not mèrely acting strangely. I think she may have actually lost it, full-blown *One Flew Over the Cuckoo's Nest* style.

"I've been thinking a lot..." she begins.

In my experience thinking rarely leads to being born again. Something bigger is happening here.

"And?" I prompt her.

"I've had a lot on my mind," she says.

"I guess it's a good thing since you've been thinking," I say slowly.

"Do you always have to be so sarcastic? It's really unbecoming."

"You have your ways of landing your billionaires. I have mine."

She winces at my joke, and I feel a twinge of panic in my stomach. Is this where she lowers the boom? Is she about to admit to me that Becca is Nathaniel West's daughter? Is she about to admit to me that I am, too?

"There's something I need to tell you," she says in a strangled voice. "You need to know. I shouldn't have kept it from you for this long. I thought it was for the best, but..."

Oh, shit.

Shit.

Shit.

Shit.

Shit.

"It's about your father."

Shit.

This is not happening. Some part of me reverts back to being five years old and I have to resist the temptation to plug my ears so I can't hear what she's saying.

"We've split up," she says finally. I could swear I hear a record screech to a halt.

"Yeah, years ago." It's official. My mom has had a psychotic break. She's clearly forgotten the last eight years of her life, seeing as she can't remember she's remarried to a pedophiliac scumbag, but remarried none the less, and that I'm too old for Happy Meals.

"Not *your* father," she says with emphasis. "Your stepfather."

That's a clarification that should have been part of the original thrust of the argument. "Good. He's slime."

"Emma!" She says reproachfully, but her expression softens and my heart sinks. "I know what he did to you. I know what he did to Becca."

And just like that, a dam bursts inside of me. I haven't cried to my mom since I ... I don't think I ever cried to my mom. The idea that she found out and took action is baffling and reassuring at the same time. It's a gesture I didn't know I needed her to make. Now that she has, that only leaves one more thing. "He belongs in jail."

"Yes, but..."

There's always a *but*.

"Out with it mom. What did he buy you with?" I shouldn't expect more, but I suppose it's not too far-fetched that a woman who would leave her husband for what he did to her daughter would also want his ass in prison. But how could he pay alimony from a cell? Plus, there's the issue of how it will look to those on the outside. A divorce is hardly unprecedented in the land of filth and money, but scandal should be avoided when possible.

"That's unfair Emma. I had to think about both of us. About our financial well-being."

"And our reputations?" I add.

"He's forgoing the prenuptial agreement. I get half of everything."

"Do you get half of his guilt?" I spit back.

Nothing could ever make me feel more disgusting than when Hans von Essen admitted to me that he'd molested my sister for years. He could claim it was mutual all he wanted but in the eyes of the law, and in mine, it was rape. Although the fact that my mother can overlook this comes pretty close to that sickening.

"Emma, you have to think about the consequences, how it will affect all of our lives if this comes out."

"Yes, I wouldn't want to destroy his career making crappy movies."

"This isn't about his career," she shoots back.

"Then what is it about, Mom? Explain it to me."

No one has held Vivian von Essen accountable for far too long. It's a little tragic that it has to be her daughter that finally does it.

"I don't want your sister to remembered that way."

"As a victim?" I ask her. "Because newsflash, she's

already a victim. She's already remembered that way. Don't try to make this about anything more than the fact that you want to save face."

"And so what if I do?" she admits haughtily. Fire sparks in her eyes, bringing some life back to her weary appearance.

"What about the other girls, Mom?"

"What other girls," she asks in horror. She could always play the naïve ingénue on command.

"The other girls he's done this to," I explain to her. "Do you think Becca was the only one? Do you think I was a fluke? How many girls have found themselves on his casting couch?"

Tales of movie producer's ethics have always been the stuff of legends. There's no doubt in my mind that Hans had all too eagerly embraced that perk of his power.

"He told me there were no others," she says too quickly. She's not lying, but she knows that he is.

"Whatever helps you sleep at night."

"Look," she says, shifting tactics, "A trust fund has been set up in your name."

"I don't care."

"There's $10 million in it."

"I don't care," I repeat. "He can't buy my silence."

"You'll never have to worry about money."

One way or another I'm not going to have to worry about money without taking Hans' dirty money. "I don't need his money. After all, think of the other trust funds I might be privy to."

"I don't know what you mean," she says.

"I know about Becca. I know why Dad settled with Nathaniel West all those years ago." I take a deep breath and ask the one question I'm not sure I want an answer to. "What I don't know is whether or not Nathaniel West is my father?"

It takes a second for my query to process through the shock frozen over her classic features.

"No, he's not," she tells me, but the pit in my stomach doesn't close.

How am I supposed to trust her when her idea of nurture has been telling me lies? Even now, she prefers the trussed-up lie to the ugly truth. Could she even admit it to me if Nathaniel was my father? "I think you should go."

"Emma, I need to know that you aren't going to tell anyone."

"I'm not," I interrupt her. I'm fighting too many battles right now to take on one more, especially one that should be hers.

"Thank you," she begins, but I stop her.

"You should be the one talking to the authorities. To the media. To everyone." I cross the room and dig a business card out of my purse, then I wait by the door until she gets the memo. She pauses at the threshold and I hand her the card.

"Agent Mackey, "she reads, shaking her head. "Oh, Emma."

"You'll just love her," I promise. "Isn't it convenient I know an FBI agent?"

"I think you should talk to him," Josie announces the next day.

"Who?" I ask in confusion. "Maddox?"

Even Marion had begun to question having a safety detail parked outside her house at all hours. Personally, I'd taken to grabbing him Starbucks when I went out on errands. Considering Maddox doesn't get involved unless he's needed—and he hasn't been—he's a bit more like having a faithful guard dog. Plus, I've discovered, his bark is worse than his bite. He might look like a pit-bull but secretly he has the heart of an English bulldog. A little dumb and very lovable.

"Not Maddox. Jameson."

"Oh, him." Josie is probably right. I should talk to him. It's the rational thing to do, which is why I'm not doing it. Not a single aspect of my life falls into rational or logical at the moment. Why should he?

"Your mom told you that Nathaniel isn't your father."

"And you believe her?" I ask. "Because everything she says is so credible.

"I don't really have a reason not to believe her. She admitted that Becca was Nathaniel's."

"Here's a better question: does she even know who my dad is?" It seems my mom had spent the late 90's bed hopping. "My dad could be anyone."

"Your dad is your dad," Josie corrects me. "*My* dad could be anyone."

"Sorry, Jos. I didn't mean to make you feel bad." According to Marion, Josie's dad was a visiting businessman who gave her a bogus name and a bogus occupation. When she tried to track him down she discovered that the company he worked for didn't exist. "You know, I've been thinking your mom probably could've paid someone at the hotel to give her the registration information on the sly."

Josie shakes her head quickly. "Don't ever suggest that to her," she advises me. "Mom's feelings on it are pretty strong. She says that if he wanted her he wouldn't have lied to her in the first place, and..."

Neither of us have to finish that thought out loud. If he hadn't wanted Marion, he definitely didn't want Josie. Given the generally disappointing men I'd encountered in my life I'd say the Deckard women were both better off.

"Don't let your mom ruin what you have with Jameson," Josie interrupts my thoughts, bringing me back to the topic--one that I'd been trying to avoid.

"The fact that he might be my brother is what might ruin things with Jameson." I practically spell it out for her.

"Well, then he deserves to know too."

"Josie, we didn't do it, but we did other stuff," I say, striving to maintain some delicacy, "and you know, I just ... I don't want him to be thinking about ..."

"You don't want to wreck it?" she guesses.

"What if he starts thinking about the fact that I might be his sister and then if I'm not, he can't look at me."

"Psychologists don't analyze things this much, Em."

"You're probably right." I'd grant her that but it doesn't mean I'm going to call him.

"Um, are we expecting company?" Josie asks, pausing the TV so that we can both hear the car pulling into her driveway. We wait for a minute, half expecting it to turn around but it doesn't.

"Maybe it's Maddox. Probably wants to go on a caffeine run." I hop up and go to the window, but it's not Maddox's familiar black sedan parked out front. It's a tiny, gold convertible. The kind of ostentatious car that only one person I know could pull off driving.

"If I were you I'd hide," I tell Josie. "The Wicked Bitch of the West has come to call."

"Life was so much simpler six months ago," Josie says with a sigh, scrambling off the couch to seek sanctuary in her room.

"And yet you're the one who wants me to call Jameson."

"If you call him maybe my house won't be Grand Central Station," she yells before she shuts the door.

"Hormones much?" I say to the now empty living room.

I save Monroe the humiliation of having to come inside a 2-bedroom house and meet her outside. Judging from the fact that she hasn't gotten out of the car she already views this as a self-service errand. Her worst half, Sabine, glowers at me from the passenger seat.

"I see you're back from LA," I say, conversationally. Sabine doesn't reply.

She doesn't talk. She just exists.

Monroe pushes her Louis Vuitton sunglasses to the tip of her nose and looks me up and down. "You're alive."

"Thanks for the info." Whatever tenuous truce that Monroe and I had managed earlier this summer is fraying at both ends. She's never liked me, and I have the kind of dirt that could destroy her. She's not ready to let the cat out of the bag on her escort empire. What she doesn't know, though, is what I found out about who killed Nathaniel West. The information Mackey gave me points suspicion for the murder at Nathaniel's own daughter.

Since I know it wasn't me, she's the next possible suspect. The trouble is that the evidence doesn't match up. If Monroe really has been passing her free time working as an escort for an exclusive Las Vegas agency, then it doesn't seem likely that she had any remnants of virginity to shed on a towel after the murder. But this is a city based on illusion. One where you can win big, play with magic, and live without consequence. Have I ever seen the real Monroe West?

"Paging Emma Southerly," Monroe says. "My brother requests that you turn your cell phone on."

"My cell phone is on," I tell her dryly.

"Then unblock him." She smacks her steering wheel so hard that the horn honks.

"I don't see why it matters to you. I'd think you'd be glad to be rid of me."

"I like to keep my frenemies close," she informs me. "Plus he's impossible to live with. He's either moping or throwing shit. There is literally no in-between. He broke mom's Baccarat vase yesterday. She's going to have him arrested. Call him."

She flicks a platinum blonde strand of hair over her shoulder.

"I'll think about it," I tell her.

"He doesn't like you staying here," she continues, "and I can see why."

"Not enough room for the servants?"

Monroe's eyes narrow into slits. "He requests that you stay at one of our other residences."

"Our?" I repeat. When did I get inducted into the West hall of infamy? "I'll think about it, *sis*."

"Whatever. I'm just the messenger." Apparently, this is the new form of passing notes in class. Send your bitchy sister to handle the situation.

"It must've taken a lot for you to lower yourself to that position." I lean down on the door and drop my voice to a whisper. "Then again, you know all about lowering your-self into positions, don't you?"

"Come home," she says, with a wicked smile that displays two rows of sparkling white teeth, "so I can teach you to fight like a West. You need practice."

She throws the car into reverse, barely giving me enough time to jump back before she peels out of the drive-way, leaving nothing but the glimmer of a Mercedes logo in her wake.

I GO to the only place where I know I'll never be judged. The graveyard is silent. The grounds-keeper must have been through recently, because the stones are swept free of dead grass clippings, artificial flowers are tucked neatly into their urns, and the whole place feels more like a museum of the dead than a cemetery. I sit at the end of Becca's grave and stare at her stone. Even now, those dates don't make sense to me.

"It doesn't feel real," I say to the wind. "How can I be 18? How can I be older than you?"

The brutality of that fact is one reason why I'm glad my birthday has been overshadowed by other events this year. Josie is busy weighing her options. Mom is focused on the divorce proceedings. On the off chance that Jameson remembers, his call can't get through to me anyway.

Even though I don't want to celebrate with other people, I pluck a Hostess cupcake out of my bag. This had been a tradition of mine and Becca's since we were kids. The other would stash the individually wrapped treat when dad remembered to get groceries, then present it like the holy grail. It was our job to remember each other's birthdays. Too many times to count, that one tiny snack cake had been our official birthday cake. As we got older, Marion took charge, picking up a small sheet cake from the grocery store and having our names put on it. But we'd kept this tradition alive quietly. It was a signal that we had each other, and that no matter how bad our family might get, we'd never lose that.

Now it's my job to remember for the both of us. I unwrap it, but I can't bring myself to eat a bite. Behind me footsteps crunch along the dry, sun-burnt grass, and I turn. The appearance of my dad at my sister's grave shouldn't be a shock, but as far as I know, he's never actually been here before.

"Hey, Pumpkin. I thought I might find you here." He nods to the cupcake. "Do you want me to sing you Happy Birthday?"

Tears prick at the corners of my eyes, but I do my best to blink them back. When I had said our birthdays were often forgotten, I should have clarified that it was mom who remembered when someone bothered. Dad? He was always a few days late. His apologies generally came with something gift wrapped from behind the counter at Pawnography.

"Do you mind if I sit down?" he asks.

I shrug, afraid to betray any more emotions.

"I'll take that as a yes." He groans as he settles onto the ground beside me.

"You can have it." I offer the cupcake to him.

"It's your birthday, kiddo. I can't believe you're 18."

He remembered my birthday, and he even got the year right. Color me plum surprised. I force myself to turn and look at him. By all accounts, he's been a lackluster father. His greatest accomplishment has been keeping a roof over our heads, which given the nature of Las Vegas and Belle Mère was actually something to brag about with his gambling addictions.

"You know, you could come home with me," he offers. "Your mom says you've been staying with Josie."

"You've been talking to mom, huh?" I wonder what else she's told him.

"I know about the divorce," he says, reading my mind.

"You can have the money," I say flatly. "Use it to expand the store or something."

"I don't want the money. I want you to be happy. Is there anything else you need to tell me?" Our eyes meet. I know what he's asking me now. It isn't like my mother to walk away from a cushy situation, especially given that Hans spent most of his time in Los Angeles, giving her free run of her own private Palm Springs resort. He suspects there's more to the story.

We stare each other down, but he doesn't push me for the information. I'm more surprised because, although he's the one seeking answers, I'm the one who finds them.

"We have the same eyes," I say softly.

"Yep. You got that from me, kiddo." He looks away then, as if the reality of what we're saying is too painful to face.

"Why didn't you tell me about Becca?" I ask him in a low voice as if she might be able to hear us talking about her.

"You two were young." His voice grows distant as he remembers. "I told myself that I would tell you when you were older, when you could understand."

"What did mom tell herself?"

"She didn't want to say anything. She said it wasn't important."

"It was important enough to sue Nathaniel West over," I choke out.

"People do stupid things when they're hurt, Em. You know that better than anyone."

"That doesn't mean I understand it," I say softly.

"You want the real answer? I guess I never told you because admitting it to you two meant admitting it to myself. When the lawyers finished fighting over the details, they sealed the records. We signed affidavits. At first it was easy to convince myself not to tell because I couldn't legally, and then it was easier to ignore it. But, you know, I realized something? Maybe a bit too late, but I realized it nonetheless. It never really mattered. Becca was my daughter, your sister. She carried my name, even if she didn't have my eyes."

"Sometimes I feel like I didn't know her at all," I admit to him.

"You knew her better than anyone." I want to tell him this isn't true, that it couldn't be. I want to spill the secrets she kept.

"There are things that I'm finding out about her now," I begin.

"You know the funny thing about lies?" Dad interrupts. "Sometimes we don't mean to lie to other people. Sometimes we're too busy lying to ourselves. Then, when we realize it, we feel guilty like we've pulled one over on them. Truth is, the people close to you, the people you love, they always see through it. They see you better than you see yourself. You saw Becca, just by loving her. I know what it's like to find something out, and to think it means a person's been taken away from you, but she wasn't taken away from you. She's right here." He doesn't point to her gravestone. Instead, he points directly at my chest. "She's here with both of us right now. Can't you feel her?"

I pause and wait, and ever so gradually, peace settles over me. "Yeah, I do."

We sit there for what could be minutes, or what could be hours. It doesn't really matter. When the spell is broken, he speaks. "You aren't coming home, are you?"

It's hard to get words past the lump in my throat. "No, I'm not, but I'm staying at Josie's."

"You're 18 now. It doesn't matter." Sadness softens the edges of his words. "Jameson seems like a good kid. He was right to get you out of there that night. He isn't his father. I know that."

I can only nod. If only it were that simple.

"Can I drive you to Josie's? Maybe take you to dinner?"

"That would be ..." I search for my answer, and I'm surprised when I find it. "Nice. That would be nice, Dad."

The night is starless when he drops me off at Josie's house a few hours later. The summer is already growing shorter. Autumn will be here in the blink of an eye, along with my senior year, but while everyone else is thinking about prom and college applications, I'm going to spend time worrying over paternity tests and murder investigations.

The house is quiet. I wasn't the only one to opt out of my self-imposed isolation. I find my cell phone on the kitchen island with a note. "You left this. It's been blowing up all day. Turn it on and call Mackey back."

I know what she's after. I ignored the subpoena delivered last week to Jameson's door. The one requesting a sample of my DNA. I can't keep hiding from the firing squad, and whatever magic Jameson's lawyers have worked to keep the court order from taking effect won't last forever. With or without her answers, she's not going to give up.

I turn on my phone and check my text messages. There's a couple from Josie, ending with a, "Oh, shit. Your phone is here. No wonder you aren't answering me," and an offer for a free sandwich, but that's all.

Still no response from The Dealer, who, judging from his Instagram feed, is taking a texting and posting holiday. Maybe I had played my card too early, or maybe I had started seeing things I wanted to see. Mackey's dogged pursuit of me might just be proof that sometimes we're so desperate for clues, we fabricate them for ourselves. I send one more text—to my suspect, anyway. If Mackey can badger me into a response, then it's worth employing a similar tactic.

The next call I make is purely practical.

Dominic Chambers answers on the first ring.

"Southerly," he says gruffly. He isn't expecting my call. No doubt he put more work into trying to find out about my sister, but not enough to justify the stamp on another bill. He's moved on from my tragic backstory and on to someone else's current drama.

"I don't need you to keep looking into who my sister's father is," I inform him.

"Oh." I can tell from the way he responds that he'd already stopped. "I guess I can put a bill ..."

"No. I have something else for you to do. You can bill as much as you want," I say, thinking of my unwanted trust fund. If I was going to be paid off, at least I could donate the money to a good cause.

I lay out what I want him to do, and he gives a low whistle. "That's not going to be easy."

"I know," I say, simply.

"Or cheap," he adds.

"I know."

This time I speak more forcefully. "I recently came into some money," I explain to him. "Price isn't an object."

"That's a real claim to make in a town like this, little lady."

"I'm not worried about it."

Judging from Dominic Chambers' velour jogging suits and penchant for accepting bogus baseball cards, he's the kind of guy who thinks in the hundreds instead of the millions. He'll be surprised when I suggest we meet in the thousands. "Mr. Chambers, you just won the lottery."

When I hang up with him, I make the last call. Mackey doesn't bother to answer her cell phone. No doubt it's some type of psychological maneuver on her end to make me question myself. Still, there's no turning back now. I'll know the truth even if I have to swallow it whole. When her voicemail beeps, I leave a one-line message.

"Where do I go to get my blood drawn?"

6

Nothing has changed inside Pawnography since I stopped coming to work. It's still a haven of other people's crap: old autographs, unwanted instruments, antique pistols. Jerry blinks as if he's seen a ghost.

"Emma?" he says uncertainly.

"Hey, Jerry. How's the store?" The place looks intact, but I know appearances can be deceiving. We both know what I'm really asking: how's my dad? I'd purposefully decided on my impromptu visit tonight since I knew Dad was heading home after he dropped me off at Josie's. I didn't want to get his hopes up that I'd be returning to my job. He hadn't always been the best boss, often leaving me to handle the financial affairs. I'd also been the on-call owner when Dad didn't show for a shift. While no one could argue that I hadn't learned a lot of trivial information about collectibles and forgeries, I'd been so caught up in not letting the shop go under that I'd forgotten to have a life of my own.

"We're doing pretty well." I don't miss the strain in his words.

"And Dad?" I might as well get to the point.

"He's been on it," Jerry says to my surprise. "But we've been busier than normal. I guess a lot of people read about you on the Internet and..."

"People came here to see me?" Seriously, I'm only accused of murder. I'm not that famous.

"Yeah. Jake's really stepped up," he says in a lowered voice as a few tourists step through the front door. "But we could use a little help."

Gee, can I sign autographs at the same time?

"That's why I came by," I say.

"Thank god. We're really missing having you here and I know your dad will be so happy. He misses you."

I suspect Jerry misses me, too. He's been in love with me since my dad hired him out of community college a few years ago. Although he's never said it, it's written across his face even now. I feel like I'm letting them both down now, because I'm not here to offer my services. I square my shoulders and deliver the bad news.

"I'm not looking for a job." I'm too busy dodging indictments. "But my friend Josie could use a part-time gig. I came by to see if you could afford to hire her."

Jerry's face falls but he recovers his pride quickly. "That would be great."

"Excellent!" My phone begins to ring in my pocket

and I back up a few steps. "I'll bring her in this week and show her the ropes."

Outside the shop I check my missed calls. I don't recognize the number but there's a voicemail.

"Call me back," Monroe orders me in the message. She really needs a life couch because her people skills are lacking. Despite that, I return the call.

"You rang?" I snap.

"Don't get your panties in a twist," she advises coolly. "I just got some news that I thought you'd be interested to hear."

"Okay," I say slowly. Monroe and I don't necessarily share the same concept of news.

"You know I don't have to go out of my way to include you."

"I'm sorry. Will you please share your news with me?" I pretend to plead, but neither of us are buying it.

However, it must have sounded moderately sincere because she continues. "Leighton woke up from her coma yesterday."

"Oh my god," I breathe. "Is she alright?"

The doctors hadn't been certain she would recover fully the last I had heard. After the trauma she'd experienced, they couldn't judge the extent of the brain damage.

"I guess," Monroe says.

I refrain from reminding her that Leighton is supposed to be one of her best friends. Mostly because my own interest is far from selfless. "Has she said anything about that night?"

"I don't know, but I think we need to find out."

"Wouldn't want anyone to find out you lied," I accuse.

"Play nicely if you want answers," Monroe warns me.

"Can she have visitors?" I ignore her rebuke. I didn't lie about that night but I didn't correct the story Monroe fed the authorities. If Leighton is awake, there's no telling what she remembers or who she has told.

"I'll meet you at the hospital in half an hour," Monroe says and hangs up. Apparently, I'm not the only one who wants to know if Leighton is talking.

I don't spot Monroe's gold convertible in visitor parking, but knowing her she has a private parking space reserved in her name. Heading inside, I pause at the information desk.

"My friend just woke up from a coma, and I was told I could visit her."

The attendant gives me a doubtful look but turns toward her computer screen and asks for the name. If Monroe was with me, we'd already be in Leighton's room. I glance around the waiting area but she's nowhere to be found.

"Visiting hours are nearly over," she informs me.

I force a tight smile. My questions can't wait for tomorrow morning.

"She can have visitors but only if you're on the approved list." The attendant studies me over the top of her wire-rim glasses. "Are you on the approved list?"

"She is," a voice answers behind me. A male voice. A familiar male voice. A voice that makes my heart leap into my throat and my stomach bottom out at the same time.

You've been played.

I should have known better than to fall for Monroe's sudden concern for a friend. Pivoting slowly around, I face the last person I want to see and the person I want to see the most.

Like my feelings, he's a study in contrast. His strong, chiseled jawline looks as if it's been expertly carved from marble even as his coppery, brown hair falls over his eyes. The loosened tie and suit jacket are at odds with the hopeful smirk creeping over his lips, and the placid depths of his gray eyes flash with lightning as our gaze meets.

I want to kiss and I want to smack him at the same time. Instead I stand there, dumbfounded.

"Come with me," he commands, taking me by the arm and hauling me toward the elevator.

Normally I would push back at the bossy gesture, but I can't think with his skin touching mine, even in such an innocent touch. We step inside and stare at the doors as they shut. I should step away and put some distance between us but I can't seem to will my body to move. When the doors slide open, he presses his hand to the small of my back and guides me into the corridor.

I refrain from melting into a puddle over the gesture. Barely.

It's easier to get to Leighton's room now that she's out of the ICU. Although judging from the harried look on the nurse's face, we aren't the only ones who've come to visit. I wonder just how many people are on the approved list of visitors. Leave it to hospital staff not to share the joy when someone wakes up from a coma.

"Sign here," the nurse says pertly, "and I'll need to see some identification."

"I thought she was getting out of the ICU," I grumble as I dig my driver's license out of my purse. They hadn't asked for ID the first time I visited her.

"New policy," she tells us. "The police suspect that her accident might have been purposeful."

It seems that Leighton has been talking. I want to tell her that the accident was actually a lie, and that I know because I was the other girl who went through the window that night, but Jameson steps in before I confess. Flashing her a crooked grin, he passes her his ID.

She glances at it, and then her eyes widen. He might be everyone's favorite suspect in the murder of the century, but his family's contributions to Belle Mère Hospital are the stuff of legend. The Wests had built more than one wing of the institution, judging by the names and plaques displayed everywhere I look. They were the reason the hospital could afford to have nurses in the first place.

"I'm sorry, Mr. West," she stammers, blushing furiously. "Go right in."

"If that's how they treat you when they think you're a murderer," I say under my breath as we turn.

"The adjective billionaire somehow mitigates whatever noun follows it." He steers me down the hall until we're in front of room forty-seven. The door opens and a middle-aged woman steps out, her red-rimmed eyes completely undermining all the plastic surgery she's undergone. She swipes at tears and smiles widely.

"Jameson!" she says fondly. Apparently, my would-be boyfriend gets around in the middle-age social circles.

"Mrs.—" he begins.

"Cheryl," she stops him with a hug. "Isn't it wonderful?"

"Yes. We've been praying for this moment." He's indulging her. The small display of charm he'd put on for the nurse turns into an entire charismatic show. I've never seen him like this, except when we first met. It hits me like a semi-truck: he's flirting with her. It might piss some girls off, but I just stand back and let him work his magic. "Can I introduce my girlfriend, Emma Southerly?"

I swallow at the term of endearment. So, Jameson West still thinks of me as his girlfriend? Does it matter? Judging from the butterflies whirling around my stomach, it matters a lot.

A shadow passes over Cheryl's face but she recovers admirably. "Of course. I know your mother."

And not my father, I add silently. I've always loved my name but right now I'm reminded that it carries a history with it that's not entirely my own. I can't help but wonder which tragedy she's recalling in her head: my alcoholic father, my parents' divorce, or my sister's death. All of them seem like the kind of low-hanging fruit, someone like her would take a bite from.

We continue our pleasantries until Cheryl pops her

head in the door. "Frank, Leighton has some visitors. Let's give them a moment with her." She turns back to us. "It will give me a chance to get some food in him. He hasn't left her side since she woke up. He's almost as bad as her boyfriend. I should warn you that she doesn't remember everything. The doctor says it will come back with time."

"Her boyfriend," Jameson repeats, zeroing in on that small aside, and I can't help but notice how his smile tightens.

Cheryl winks at him. "She couldn't moon after you forever."

I shoot Jameson a meaningful look. Apparently, he'd left out some bits about his relationship to his younger sister's bestie.

"Don't be jealous Duchess. She was just some kid who always hung around when I was home," he whispers as Leighton's mother ducks into the room for her purse.

"I was just some kid hanging around," I remind him tartly.

"Jealousy suits you," he teases.

Before I can give him more grief about how many of my peers he's strung along with his impish smile, we're welcomed in to her room. There are less machines tracking her every heartbeat and breath. A dozen fresh flower arrangements take up every flat surface. No doubt well wishes from her numerous pals who sent flowers rather than interrupt their Mediterranean summer holidays. Before when I'd visited the room felt cold and sterile, but now it's as alive as the girl sitting up in her hospital bed with a wide smile on her face. But she's not looking at us. Instead her gaze is fixed on her boyfriend.

Hugo Roth can barely tear his eyes away from her as if she might vanish, but he nods a hello.

"We'll leave you kids alone," Cheryl calls, tugging her husband out the door.

Kids. The repeated use of the term annoys me. We aren't kids anymore. Our childhood was stolen by this city and its sins. Pretending that we're going to have some Leave It to Beaver catch-up session is as naïve as believing you could raise us kids here in the first place.

"Hey," I say awkwardly by way of greeting as the door shuts behind them.

Leighton blinks owlishly as if her vision needs adjustment. Then she realizes she's not seeing things. "Hi...Emma."

"I hope you don't mind us stopping by." Jameson interjects himself before things can get any weirder.

Maybe I should have brought her flowers. I could have played the part of concerned friend better and she might have thought she'd forgotten our relationship. As it is, whatever Leighton can't remember, she knows I don't belong here.

"Of course not." She waves him off with a tired hand. "I'm surprised. I expected to see a West today, just not..."

She trails off and I know what she's hinting at. She didn't expect to see Jameson. Not when she's spent the last three years being Monroe West's pet sidekick.

"I'm not certain my sister has heard yet," Jameson lies smoothly.

"Ugh." Leighton smacks the plastic, hospital mattress with an audible thwack. "My parents are being tyrants about letting me have my phone. I've had to use Hugo's."

At the mention of his name, Hugo startles out of his reverie and runs his hand over his spiky hair. "Sorry, guys. What?"

"Your girlfriend was just telling us about your chivalry," I say dryly. As of a few months ago, Hugo's reputation as a party boy had been intact. I'd witnessed his devotion to her firsthand the night that Nathaniel West died when he'd been surrounded by a gaggle of freshmen girls. "I didn't know you two were dating."

"We weren't." Leighton flushes. "Not really."

"And now?" I ask pointedly. Hooking up while one party was unconscious seems like a strange way to start a relationship. But what do I know? My romance is the result of needing an alibi.

"Things are different," Hugo says as if that settles it. I open my mouth to press the point but he shuts me up by adding, "I'm sure you both understand how quickly things change."

That I did.

"Tell me," Hugo continues, shirking some of the facade of respectability. "Are the rumors true?"

"Which ones?" Jameson asks with the practiced air of a tycoon's son.

"All of them. Murder of the century is quite the accomplishment," he says with a smirk.

So much for no one reading the tabloids. Leighton leans forward, some color returning to her usually tan face. Apparently gossip can serve to heal as much as damage. One person's nightmare is another person's Lifetime movie of the week.

"You know better than to believe rumors." Jameson takes the interrogation in stride, but I can't help looking at the floor. Maybe someday I'll get used to being analyzed by everyone we meet, even people we already know, but today's not that day.

As it is my patience with social pleasantries is up. "Look, we came for a reason. I didn't see who pushed us through that window, but I know you did."

Jameson sighs next to me, but I ignore him. His social caste might get off on their games of cat and mouse, but I live in the real world where bluntness will suffice.

"I don't remember," Leighton says in a small voice.

It's probably best that there are still a few monitors hooked up to her, because I really want to shake an answer out of her. Instead I'll have to stick to gentle encouragement. Two traits I'm not known for.

"I remember your face right before the...accident." I decide to go with the lie. If Leighton doesn't believe she's ratting someone out maybe we'll get more out of her. "You looked happy."

"Happy?" Her voice is hollow as she repeats me. I

realize then that she's as lost as to who did it as I am. But maybe I can draw her a map.

"We were talking about someone," I remind her, taking a step forward. Out of the corner of my eye, I see Hugo stiffen and I stop. No need to upset her guard dog. "Do you remember?"

Her blue eyes are misty as she shakes her head.

Okay, I have to give her a little more to work with. "I thought I overheard you talking to Monroe about Jameson, but you told me you were talking to her about Jonas."

"Jonas?" Hugo says. "What does he have to do with anything?"

"That's what I'm trying to figure out." My words grate off my tongue as I try to hold on to gentle or encouraging—and fail.

"I don't remember," she says miserably.

"She just woke up," Hugo reminds us.

If I'd just woken up from a coma after some psycho pushed me out a window, I'd be screaming his or her name until they were under arrest. But comme ci, comme ça.

"I don't think Jonas was the one who pushed us." There's an apology written in her voice.

"Was he even in town?" Jameson asks and I realize I'd left my boyfriend out of my manic, conspiracy theories.

"Yeah, he wasn't on my list either until..."

"Until what?" Hugo's face darkens. Apparently in the war between the girl he loves and his best friend, Hugo's already taken sides.

"Until I saw this." I pull up the screen shot of The

Dealer's Instagram account on my phone. "He erased this but I took a picture."

"That's Josie," Jameson points out in a quiet voice.

"Yeah, but she's not the only one in the picture," I inform them, not bothering to smother my annoyance. No one had been safe from The Dealer's unwanted attention this summer and he'd used that to his advantage. We'd all been too distracted by analyzing the people in the photos to notice something like a reflection.

"I never saw this photo," Hugo says slowly.

"The Dealer deleted this photo, and there's a reason." They pass my phone around, studying the picture. No one speaks, which is how I know that they all see exactly what I saw.

"Why is Jonas posting pictures as The Dealer?" Hugo asks.

"Who's The Dealer?" Leighton's confusion is excusable since she's been in a coma.

"Someone's been posting pictures." I explain the whole thing to her, but it doesn't seem like she processes it. I've known her long enough that I'm not certain if her slowness is the result of her injuries or her IQ. But before I can explain anymore, Hugo is on his feet.

"Where are you going?" I ask as he leans down and kisses Leighton's head in a gesture of farewell.

"I need to talk to my best friend." He pushes past me, and I shoot a pleading look to Jameson. He takes the hint and follows him.

"What's happening?" Leighton cries out.

I'm torn between running after them and comforting her. "I think I just started a fight."

"Emma, he isn't the one who pushed us," she says firmly. "You can't let Hugo attack him. He'll never forgive himself."

"How can you be so certain?" If there's one thing I've learned this summer, it's that people aren't always what they seem.

"Because I remember why I was talking to Monroe about Jonas."

"And?" I demand.

"I can't tell you, but he's not the one. He couldn't be."

There's enough certainty in her words to make me doubt my own cynicism, but if I give that up, what will I have left?

7

Jameson weaves in and out of traffic, trying to keep up with the taillights of Hugo's Porsche. I'm torn between my desire to batter him with questions and my need to clutch the armrest for dear life.

"Why didn't you tell me about Jonas? About the picture?" His eyes flicker over to mine before returning to the pursuit.

"We haven't really been talking," I remind him through clenched teeth.

"And why is that, Duchess? Why are you avoiding me?"

I gasp as he narrowly misses a car pulling into traffic. "That's kind of complicated."

"I'm listening."

"I'd rather you drive, West," I hiss as he swerves into another lane. "Does he even know where he's going?"

We're not on the way to Jonas's house, but Hugo

hadn't hesitated when he went flying out of the hospital parking lot. I'd barely slammed my door shut before we had to take off after him.

"Don't change the subject," Jameson warns me. "I've been patient, but if you wanted out, you could have told me."

"Out?" I repeat. As if whatever this was between us could ever be that easy. "Why would you think that?"

I'm in love with you. My heart pounds against my chest as if trying to break free of the cage I'm keeping it in. It hurts like hell to hold the words back, but I know I have to until I know the truth.

Jameson slams on the brakes and I'm surprised to see we're parked in front of the Belle Mère gymnasium. He shuts off the engine and dares one look at me. "Because why else would you want to hurt me?"

He's out of the car and heading inside after Hugo before I can process what he's said. Tears sting my eyes. I want him to understand. I want to explain why I've stayed away, but how can I? Either way, I'm destined to hurt him.

"Now is not the time," I coach myself. It takes a good deal of effort to climb out of the car, but once my feet hit the pavement I'm running toward the double doors. I have no idea what anyone is doing here so late, but the school must not be locked up. Or Jonas has a key.

The scene that greets me looks as if it's been staged. Jonas is frozen, basketball in hand, in the middle of the court with Hugo stopped a few feet away, screaming so loudly that I can't understand him. Jameson glances at me from the door frame.

"Should we jump in?" I ask, my nerves rattled by Hugo's fury.

"Give it a sec," he advises, but we move closer. Jonas glances to us as if we might be able to explain what's happening. But when my eyes meet his, Jonas turns away. It's enough to confirm my suspicions. I'd given him a chance to come forward to me privately, offering him an out via text message, but he hadn't taken it. Now he has to face the consequences.

"I don't know what you're asking me, man." Jonas manages to punctuate Hugo's screams with a response.

"Did you push her?" Hugo repeats, enunciating each word carefully.

"Who?" Jonas looks genuinely confused, but its neither a denial or a confession and Hugo is here for one or the other.

Hugo lunges at his best friend, knocking the ball out of his hands and sending them both flying into a heap.

"Who?" Jonas screams, but the repeated question is met with a right hook to his face.

"Did you push Leighton?" Hugo demands as we rush over to break up the fight, but before we reach them he's started punching Jonas again.

"I wasn't the one who pushed her." Jonas's answer is nearly lost as Hugo pummels him.

He doesn't fight back, so by the time Jameson hauls Hugo off of him, Jonas's face is already swelling from the repeated impact. Scrambling away from the court, Jonas slumps against the wall and wipes the back of his hand over his bloody lip. He inspects it for a second as if he's surprised. "Let him go."

"I don't think that's a good idea." Jameson's grip on Hugo doesn't loosen.

"He's my best friend," Jonas says, "and I trust him to let me tell my side of the story. I wasn't the one who pushed Leighton."

"It's your funeral," Jameson mutters before he drops his hold on Hugo. Despite the rage radiating from Hugo, he stays still. I expected Hugo to pounce again. Even after his change of heart this summer, I didn't think Hugo could help but allow himself to be more than a mass of impulses, especially given how angry he is at the moment. Apparently, Jonas does know him better than the rest of us.

"Start explaining," Hugo orders. His hands are still clenched into fists, a reminder that he could strike at any time.

"I wasn't the one who pushed Leighton," he repeats himself.

"You said that already." Hugo practically growls the words.

Letting the two of them work this out on their own is going to get us nowhere. I step forward until I'm nearly between the two of them, and Jameson frowns. I ignore his concern. We might not have been the ones throwing punches but we've been a part of the fray for a while.

"Then why would someone push us? She had something on you."

"On him?" Hugo asks, his confusion growing. He moves forward and I wedge myself further between them.

"Duchess!" Jameson calls in a low voice, but I ignore his warning.

"I overheard Leighton and Monroe talking. I thought they were discussing Jameson, but Leighton told me it was Jonas. It was the last thing she said before..." There's no need to bring up the accident again. Hugo is revved enough already. I can't bring myself to look at Jameson. He'd thought that I trusted him that night and then I'd questioned that at the first opportunity. Whatever Jonas had to tell us now better make up for all the damage he'd been doing this summer.

Hugo relaxes a bit as if he's interested in this explanation, but the color drains from Jonas's face. I can see the struggle in his eyes. There's no doubt in my mind that he knows what Leighton and Monroe were talking about that night.

"Okay, you didn't push us," I say when the silence drags on. "Did you kill Nathaniel?"

Jonas shakes his head. I believe him despite the guilt written in white across his face. Apparently, Hugo does as well, because he unballs his fists. I have the sinking suspicion that whatever he's hiding has nothing to do with us. It feels dirty and wrong to force his secrets into the open, but as long as secrets stand between us, we can't trust each other.

The trouble is that I know what it's like to hide out in the open. Jonas looks like a cornered animal, and I can't bring myself to be the one who destroys him. "Then we're done here. Whatever secret he's keeping doesn't affect us."

Jameson's head tilts in surprise as he studies me.

"You never stop surprising me, Duchess," he whispers so only I can hear him.

But my gift of amnesty doesn't mean that he can keep it trapped inside him any longer. Jonas slides to the ground, hanging his head to hide his face. The rest of us freeze, uncertain what to say. When he looks up to us, his face is tear-stained. No one speaks. It's an unspoken agreement to give him the time he needs to open up to us. After a few minutes of silence, he begins.

"Monroe knows something about me. Something no one else knows. At least no one at Belle Mère Prep. She's been keeping it a secret for a long time."

"Yeah, she's your girlfriend, man." Hugo drops to the ground beside him. Could I transition from angry to supportive that quickly, even with Josie? I hope I never have to find out. Half an hour ago, I honestly thought Hugo might kill him. Now he's practically holding his hand. Maybe he's a better friend than I am, or maybe Hugo Roth is a better person than we've—okay, I've—given him credit for.

"I'm not sure where the story begins," he admits.

I almost suggest he start with why he screwed Monroe at the freshman desert party but I keep the suggestion to myself. Will wonders never cease?

"We'll listen," Hugo says encouragingly.

Dammit, Hugo Roth really is a nice guy parading around in a pariah suit.

"Don't worry," he says to me as if he can read my mind, "I'm still a dick."

"No, you're not." Jonas's voice is almost wistful and the dreamy undertone deepens as he begins his story.

"Most of you don't know my older sister. My parents sent her off to school in London not long after I turned ten. Hugo's met her." He pauses waiting for Hugo to nod, then continues, "There's always been rumors around it. She was fourteen at the time, and well, you know my parents. They make Donald Trump look like a liberal. Most people believed she'd gotten herself in trouble."

Did people still think like that? Especially in Vegas? And what did that even mean in trouble? It seems to me that half the adults I know didn't want their own kids. Why blame a girl for getting pregnant when you did it yourself?

"She didn't do anything. She was the perfect daughter. I was the reason she got sent away. I suppose they thought that they'd better keep their real problem child close to home."

"But why send your sister away?" I blurt out before I can stop myself.

"I think that the main reason was because Jessica was my only ally in the house. She understood me and more than that, she sympathized. Our parents weren't just hard on us. They expected perfection. I was their dirty little secret. Their son that liked to play with his sister's dolls. It was easier to send the only other person that knew away. Jessica made a lot of friends there—powerful, rich friends. She's marrying some duke or baron or something next year. I haven't even met him," Jonas confesses. "I guess it was better for her to go there. Sending me away would have been a reward for what my parents saw as acting out. So, I stayed here and with Jessica and her dolls gone, they shaped me into a man, by their standards. Lacrosse, soccer. Any sport imaginable. When I hit high school, they didn't encourage me to date. They demanded it. If there was a party, I had to be there. Drinking, sex—they could forgive all my sins as long as they were red-blooded, male sins."

As he spoke pieces of Jonas that had always been a puzzle to me began to click into place. When we'd dated, he hadn't breached the second base barrier. Being with him had been warm and comfortable. Of course, I'd been smitten as a kitten. What girl wouldn't have fallen for the second coming of Justin Bieber at that age? When he'd gotten together with Monroe, I assumed he'd wanted sex and she'd been a more willing participant. That's how I'd wound up in his best friend's bed trying to prove something to myself. But maybe Jonas hadn't wanted to have sex with me...or her. But if that was the case, why had he?

"It was fine for a while. I had a girlfriend that didn't mind making out, and she was nice. She never pushed me for more, and I don't think she suspected who I really was." His eyes stray over to mine, and I can see the silent apologies in them. "And then I screwed up, and Monroe West was there to catch me as I fell."

"Monroe has never caught anyone," Jameson says coolly.

"I don't mean that she helped me," Jonas clarifies. "She saw my indiscretion as an opportunity. She had a secret of her own, which she revealed to me along with some pretty damning cell phone photos. It was my worst nightmare but she gave me an out. She wanted the whole school to know that she was taken. All I had to do was get drunk and screw her at a party with enough witnesses."

"Why?" The question I've wanted him to answer for years slips out, but I'm not the one asking. Hugo is.

"It was the perfect alibi. I knew it would get back to my parents, and that in their own messed up rationale, they would think they fixed me. Do you know how fucked it is when your dad pours you a whiskey and slaps you on the back for something like that? I mean, they bought me a car. As far as they were concerned, I was normal again. All I had to do was sell my soul to Monroe."

"What did she have on you?" Hugo demands. Jonas is skirting the issue, and even though all the clues are there, we all need to hear him say it.

"I was drunk. I spent a lot of my time my freshman year drunk. It was easier to cope most of the time. Emma usually came to the parties with me, but she stayed home for some reason." He looks at me to see if I remember. I do. I'd gone out with Becca that night. Jonas had acted strangely after that night. Every day it felt as if he was going through the motions. I'd expected him to dump me, but he'd chosen a far more humiliating and hurtful way to end our relationship.

"I remember," I say softly, and try as I might, I can't place any forgiveness in my words.

"I didn't know what I was doing when I kissed him." Jonas barely pauses to let the truth sink in before he goes on. "He was drunk, too. More drunk than I was, but even as I did it, I knew I was lying to myself. He was straight and he probably would have kicked my ass if he knew what I did. I barely remembered it myself. I thought maybe I'd dreamed it until Monroe showed up with photographic evidence. She left it up to me. I could help her cover up her own secret and ensure that no one found out the truth or she could blast the proof all over Facebook. I didn't know what my parents would do if they found out, but, honestly, I was more ashamed. I didn't want to lose my friends. So, I went along with it. I am truly sorry, Emma."

His words work like alchemy, melting the cold, stoniness in my heart and creating acceptance. I'd held onto my grudge against him long enough, tricking myself into believing it was merely unrequited love. "I forgive you."

"Are you saying you're gay?" Hugo asks in a strangled voice.

Jonas takes a deep breath as if to steady himself. "Yes, I am. I'm s—"

"Why are you sorry?" Hugo cuts him off. "It's not a big deal, man."

Another moment of acceptance and maybe Jonas can

finally shake free of the fear that's crippled him for so long, but the terror lingers in his eyes.

"I need to tell you something." His voice is shaky and my breath catches as realization dawns on me. Jameson grips my arm as if he senses my urge to interrupt this confession before Jonas gets hurt.

"It was you," Jonas admits. "Monroe caught me kissing you."

Hugo's eyes widen and then he does the last thing I expect: he laughs. "I'm flattered. If I played for that team... well, you know."

"You're not pissed?" The tension in Jonas's body relaxes and he practically slumps to the floor. He'd been bracing himself for a fight.

"Look, you've seen me drunk. I doubt you're the only guy I've kissed." Hugo continues to roll with it. "I get why you didn't tell me, but I don't understand why you had to be The Dealer."

I suck in a breath and wait for his response. Jonas might have less to atone for than I previously thought, but this was thing I wanted to understand.

"It's simple, really. The whole world was going crazy. I saw all of you there that night, and I was so tired of hiding who I was. Those pictures all tell more of a story than you think. That one of you"—he looks to Hugo— "carrying that girl? You just made sure she laid down on a bed."

That wasn't the conclusion I'd drawn when I saw it. That photo might have been innocent but what about the others. What story was he trying to tell? "And the others?"

"It's felt like karma has been on vacation for too long in Belle Mère."

"So you took over her job?" I guess.

"Someone had to. I know that whoever killed Nathaniel West was there that night. It was the perfect opportunity to hold people accountable."

"While still hiding," I bite out.

"I guess it's what I'm good at," he says in a flat voice.

"So you don't know who did it?" I ask. "Who killed Nathaniel?"

"Not any more than you do." He shakes his head and I feel myself deflate. So, Jonas thinks I'm innocent, but he has no way to prove it. He also has no idea who is responsible. We're back to square one.

Hugo stands up, brushing off his jeans, before he hauls Jonas to his feet. We stand awkwardly around each other, none of us certain what to say. After a minute, Jameson tugs at my hand. I step closer and he whispers in my ear, "Let's give them some space."

That's exactly what we should do. The answers aren't here, and the healing that needs to be done has nothing to do with us. But leaving them here will give Jameson exactly what he wants: me—alone.

A devilish grin curves across his mouth, and I know he has me right where he wants me.

8

I wait until we're out of the school before I lower the boom. "Jameson, I have to go."

He steps in front of me blocking my exit. There are about twelve ways out of Belle Mère Prep and I know all of them, but somehow I don't doubt that Jameson will beat me to each exit.

"We need to talk, Duchess, you can't keep hiding from me." This time he doesn't cover the pain in his voice. He allows it to pierce his words and I feel it as acutely as I feel my own pain. "We can work through this."

I doubt it, but admitting that to him, as well as myself, means facing the truth. I want to talk. I want to explain, but I hesitate, only daring to lift my eyes to his. It's a mistake. Because what might have been an innocent gesture feels too intimate.

If Mackey's hunch is correct and Nathaniel West is my father, how can I feel this way about Jameson? More than ever, I want to believe what my mother told me. That whatever moment of insanity led to her conceiving Nathaniel's daughter, and my sister, didn't happen twice. But seeing as I've been a regular lightening rod this summer, I'm not sure I'll be that lucky. I want to be Jake Southerly's daughter. Because that obstacle—a Southerly falling for a West—feels a lot more surmountable than this.

"I know what's going on," he says, interrupting my thoughts.

"No, you don't." I shake my head, trying to clear it and things only grow hazier. Or is that the Jameson effect? I'm not really certain anymore.

"I do know." This time his tone is firm. There's no doubt that he is Nathaniel West's son. Unyielding, commanding, powerful—he got all those traits from his father.

"Jameson, I—"

But he cuts me off. "I'm not your brother."

You know that old cliché: time stands still? Well, it really fucking *can* happen. Everything around me grinds to a halt.

Jameson takes my hand, apparently unaffected by this time warp, and snaps me out of my daze.

"How? What? Why?" I stumble, looking for exactly the right question to ask.

Of course, Jameson already knows the answers. "I'm not stupid, Duchess. There are a lot of people willing to be bought in law enforcement. A little information for a lot of money isn't hard to understand when you've seen the pension plan."

"You bought someone off?" I ask in confusion. He nods, and tightens his grip on my fingers. That's both disturbing and reassuring. There's only one problem. "But I haven't taken the DNA test yet."

Did he think it would be this easy to trip me up? My anxiety and I have been friends far too long to be so easily soothed.

"I know that. I also know that you arranged to have your blood drawn at the Las Vegas Medical Clinic next Wednesday. That won't be necessary, by the way."

Confusion shifts to annoyance. "Jameson West, I am not one of your family's puppets that can be ordered about. There are no strings attached to me. If you think you're going to make me dance around, you are completely mistaken."

"You're wrong about that." He takes a step closer, until our bodies are Mère inches apart. Spicy notes of citron and sandalwood tug at latent memories that I've been trying hard to forget. "There is a string attached to you. Only one."

"And you think you can pull it?" I surmise, jutting my chin to show how wrong he is. But who are we kidding? We both know he can pull it anytime he wants. That's why I've been hiding out in my best friend's bedroom for the better part of a week.

"I'm not trying to pull your strings, Duchess. That string that I'm talking about, can't you feel it? Running between the two of us?" His thumb traces the back of my wrist, and my pulse speeds up as if he's willing it to race. "We're connected. Nothing can change that. Stop being so afraid of it."

"I'm not afraid of it!" I explode. "I'm afraid that you're my brother, and that's really, really creepy."

"I'm not," he insists.

"We won't know until next Wednesday. Actually, probably longer. I'm guessing they don't have one-step paternity tests on hand." Given the frequency the topic shows up on daytime talk shows, you'd think you could get a one-prick test at the supermarket that could tell you who your baby-daddy is in less than three minutes.

"If you'd let me finish talking to you, I could explain how I know."

I need to break the connection sizzling between us before the lightening crackling around us becomes a full-blown storm. I pull my hand away gently, allowing the regret to show on my face. I have a tendency to hide behind my bitchiness like it's my own feminist fortress, but Jameson hasn't done anything to hurt me intentionally. The sins that stand between us are those of our parents, and if he can, I'll allow him to tear them down. But while they're still up, I need the physical and emotional barriers to remain intact.

"I imagine I found out like you did. My lawyers and researchers were able to uncover the nature of the lawsuit that was settled between our parents when we were both much younger. When I read the details of your sister's paternity report, I knew what was troubling you. About the same time, a leak came through in Mackey's team, revealing that my suspicions were correct. The FBI also knew my father was your sister's father. The source also confirmed that Mackey had been in contact with you, using this information to pressure you into getting the DNA test my lawyers had worked so hard to prevent. It was easy to see why. If my father and your mother had had an affair, who's to say you also weren't his daughter?" He clears his throat. It's a small sign of discomfort, but it's there. Good to know that the thought bothered him as much as it bothered me. "But I knew you couldn't't be."

"That makes one of us," I mutter.

"I knew you'd think you were," he continues. "That's your biggest weakness. You need to have a little faith."

"In whom?" I retort. I hadn't been given a lot of opportunities to have faith in my life. My mom blowing up her marriage to my father hadn't instilled faith and love. My father's inability to keep the electricity on for more than six months at a time didn't instill a lot of faith in authority. But really, watching my sister die because of one stupid decision in a car, that's when I lost faith in the universe.

"I know you have a lot of reasons not to believe. And I know it might take you a lifetime to heal from all the terrible things that happened to you. But I'm going to be there for that lifetime. I'm going to spend every day reminding you that good things can happen. That it's okay to believe and to hope and to have faith in other people."

"What if I can't?" I ask in a breathless voice. I don't have a successful track record when it came to blind trust.

"Baby steps, Duchess." He reaches out and brushes his knuckle under my chin. "Start with me. Have some faith in me. We'll go from there."

I had faith in Jameson, and it had been taken away from me. Why can't he see that my cynicism isn't rooted in some warped fixation on the past, but in the continued barrage of unfortunate events that had both brought us together and torn us apart?

"I can't just have faith," I admit to him in a small voice. I want to, and I want to tell him that. But he'll take my foolish desires as a sign that I'm capable of this tremendous feat he's asking of me.

"How about we start with something concrete?" he says softly.

I raise one eyebrow. He's going to need a miracle if he's asking me to make this leap. Then again, I'm going to need a miracle if I plan to walk out of here alone tonight. I want him, and I want the picture he's painting. But is it a future I can ever have?

"Oh Duchess, I'm sorry they broke you." The light finger on my jaw shifts and his whole palm cups the side of my face. His touch feels warm and comforting and right, so how could it ever be wrong? "But I'm going to fix you."

"You can't." The sooner he figures that out, the better off we'll both be.

"Look at me," he demands, and when I open my eyes, his burn into mine. "I'm Jameson West, and I can do anything I want. So, when I say I'll spend my life teaching you how to have faith—when I say I'm going to fix you—I will."

I want so badly to trust him, but in my experience, dreams don't come true.

"I told you that I had proof. We'll start with one concrete reason why you should believe in us."

"And what is that?" I snap, as I feel the wounds in my heart begin to crack open.

"Your DNA," he says. "It doesn't match my father's. For good measure, it doesn't match mine, either. You aren't related to me, Emma Southerly."

I can't process what he's saying, how he knows this. He takes my silence for exactly what it is, disbelief. Sighing, he reveals the source of his findings. "You were sleeping at my house, remember? I borrowed your hairbrush, your toothbrush. Hell, there was a whole team in the guest bedroom. You could probably be cloned."

"What does that mean? How can they know so soon? Mackey said..."

"Mackey's using the resources of a government-funded laboratory. I had labs in New York, Switzerland and London test and send results. Their findings were all quite clear. We're not related. So, as to your question, what does that mean? It means that you're going to lock your car, and then you're going to get into the passenger seat of mine. My jet is waiting on standby. It's your birthday, Duchess, and I'm taking you wherever you want to go. The registered flight plan has us going to New York, but from there we can go wherever, so long as that place has a bed."

"A bed?" I choke out the word. My cheeks flush with heat as the memories I've done my best to erase flash through my mind. There's no stopping them now that Jameson has drained the fight from me.

"It's your birthday." His voice is low and suggestive. Apparently, he hasn't forgotten the date or why it is important. He had been the one to set the rule and force me to agree: we wouldn't sleep together until then. He smirks as if reading my mind. "You're 18, Duchess, and that means you're mine."

9

My hand stays tightly clutched in Jameson's until we reach the airfield. The only time I let it go is to send Josie a text that I won't be back tonight. I spot Maddox's bulky form waiting by the plane. I guess there's no way that I'm going anywhere without protection. Jameson gives me an apologetic smile as he releases my hand, but he's out of the car and around to my door before the heat of his touch has fully dissipated. This time, when his fingers knit through mine, I suspect he won't be letting go.

We climb the stairs into the main cabin of the jet together. Jameson pauses to whisper instruction to Maddox and the rest of the crew.

I've been in the West family private jet before, but that fact does nothing to lessen the excitement I feel now. Luxurious private travel had usually been available to me when it came to one route only: Las Vegas to Palm Springs and back again. Knowing this plane could take me anywhere is the best birthday present I could ever ask for.

"We're going to take off soon, Duchess." Jameson guides me to a cushy leather chair, and I laugh when he begins to buckle my seat restraint.

"I can do that myself," I assure him.

He does it anyway, kissing me on the forehead in the process. "I have to protect what's mine."

He isn't saying it, but I know the last few days of separation nearly drove him crazy. If it hadn't been for Josie, I'd probably be stark raving mad as well. It's going to take more than a few serious conversations to heal the damage that's been done to our relationship, but right now I think we're simply relieved to be together. We can piece together the events of the last week later.

Jameson takes the seat next to mine, and I raise an eyebrow when he doesn't buckle up.

"Do I need to buckle you in?" I ask.

He heaves a sigh and fastens the safety belt.

"Just protecting what's mine," I tease him. The butterflies in my stomach take flight as the jet begins to wheel down the runway.

"Are you okay?" he asks next to me, and I realize I'm clutching the arms of my seat.

"This isn't how I saw my day going," I admit. Heading on a romantic adventure hadn't been on my radar.

"Monroe packed a bag of your things that you left at my house."

I think that information is supposed to reassure me, but

I've met his sister. I can't imagine what she thinks is necessary for a weekend holiday. Beggars can't be choosers, so I cross my fingers there are clean panties. Anything else is cake.

He holds my hand until we're in the air. As soon as I feel the landing gear lock into place, I'm out of my seat, and scrambling onto his lap. Strong arms wrap around my waist as I straddle him, and I feel even safer than I did before.

"I missed you," I murmur. I can't seem to bring myself to meet his eyes because Jameson's right. I didn't have faith. I'd been the one to nearly give up on us. I can blame my crappy childhood all I want, but I chose to believe the worst.

"Look at me, Duchess," he commands in a low voice, and I dare to lift my face to his. "It's behind us now."

Such simple words, but they carry so much meaning. We'd already faced what felt like an insurmountable obstacle. Whatever comes next, I know we will have each other.

"I don't deserve you," I whisper.

"No, you deserve more."

I take a deep breath, a leap of faith, and choose to believe him.

"What have you been doing while you hid from me this week?" Jameson asks, tucking a strand of hair behind my ear.

I nuzzle against his hand. This week has been full of terrible and right now, I want to be with him.

"Talk to me," he urges. "When we were apart, I nearly went crazy wondering what you were doing."

"I was hiding from my life," I confess. My life had managed to intrude anyway, and it will keep doing so. "Let's see, my mom is getting a divorce."

Jameson's eyes darken, and I know he's thinking about the night he saved me from my stepfather. He clears his throat. "Because of what he did to you and your sister?"

I nod as I begin to feel tears pricking my eyes. "She refuses to take the information to the police."

"I can handle that," he practically growls.

"No," I say resolutely. "I could, but this isn't my battle anymore. I don't want any more to do with it. Even though..."

I hesitate, because I don't like bringing up money, especially not with a West.

"Out with it, Duchess," he commands.

"She's arranged for a trust fund in my name. Hans was more than happy to settle the separation quietly," I say. I know Jameson can read between the lines. My stepfather paid my mother off. "It's blood money."

"You don't have to take it."

I don't tell him that I've already used some for a good cause: looking into our case with a private investigator. After his miraculous feat, hiring a P.I. hardly seems like a groundbreaking contribution.

"I won't." I leave it at that. "I'll donate it. With global warming, there's always some new disaster relief fund that needs money."

"Be serious for just a second," he advises, kissing the tip of my nose.

"I am. I can't think of a better way to spend his bribe than to erase some of the bad from the world with some good."

"Whatever you think is best. Besides we don't need money."

"We?" I repeat. "When did we sign up for a joint checking account?"

It's meant as a joke but Jameson shows no signs of laughing.

"You get serious," I say, smacking his shoulder. Although all signs point to the fact that he is serious—very serious.

"Wests don't joke about money." He doesn't clarify further. Before I can push the topic, because it seems pretty important that he know I don't want his money, Maddox joins us. He's carrying a small birthday cake blazing with so many candles I half expect that he'll start a cabin fire. Without a flight attendant, I'm not certain if oxygen masks will drop down in that event.

"You don't look like a stewardess," I say when he places the cake on the table in front of Jameson and I.

"I left my pantyhose at home," he says dryly.

I don't complain when they insist on singing happy birthday to me. I turn to face the cake but remain on Jameson's lap. He sings the words softly into my left ear, and when he finishes he whispers, "Make a wish."

I don't have to, because it's already come true.

When the candles are all blown out, Maddox ducks back into the crew quarters to give us some privacy. I twist in Jameson's arms until I'm staring into his stormy eyes.

"What did you wish for, Duchess?"

"You." Then I seal my mouth to his.

It's a few hours before dawn when we arrive at the West Hotel in New York City. Perched at the top of Wall Street, it's a haven for business travelers and the elite who value privacy and luxury over nightlife. It may be the city that never sleeps but I doze in and out to the sound of trash trucks and delivery vans preparing for the busy day ahead. Despite my best attempts I couldn't keep my eyes open long enough to take in much of the city. Sight-seeing will have to come later. Right now the only sight I want to see is a pillow.

Our car pulls up to the valet station and a weary looking bellhop rushes out to meet us. I wonder if he's starting his shift or nearing the end of it. Either way I feel his pain.

"You look dead on your feet," Jameson notes as he helps me out of the Lincoln Continental that's delivered us to his family's local hotel-away-from-home.

"I'm fine." But the veracity of my claim is undermined when I immediately punctuate it with a yawn. The trouble is that I don't want to be tired. Not here. Not since Jameson and I are finally together again. "I just need some coffee."

Jameson casts a doubtful look at me. As we step inside, he pulls me close. The lobby is nearly empty save for a few staff members milling about dusting and polishing the floors. It's unlike the West Resort and Casino in Las Vegas. This hotel is that hotel's big brother: grown up, sophisticated, and aiming for partner at his law firm. Its elegance is understated, relying on subtle, but expensive décor choices. I drink in the leather club chair dotting the periphery and the black veined marble I can only assume has been imported from somewhere so far away that it cost twice as much to ship as it did buy. The West New York whispers wealth while its casino brother screams debauchery.

Whatever travel arrangements Jameson has made seem to be in order. Maddox and our driver bypass waiting with us at the front desk and go straight to the elevators.

"It will only be a minute," Jameson promises me, "and then I can get you into bed."

Bed.

The word jolts me awake faster than a triple espresso. We're going to bed. Together. And I'm eighteen.

A middle-aged man in an expensive three-piece scuttles out from the door marked private access and zeros in on us. His hands steeple together and he bobs his head as if bowing to a patriarch.

I'll never get used to these reactions. Jameson has my respect, because he's earned it. Everywhere else we go the deference he receives is born of his family name. He takes the man proffered hands smoothly, accepting the introduction while I zone out. The two can feign business talk, I have other things on my mind.

I can't help but be preoccupied what with words like bed being casually tossed about. This time when Jameson and I go to bed together there will be no push and pull. I won't peer pressure, and he won't say no. I've been planning to sleep with Jameson for months. Why am I getting so nervous now?

Probably because it's such a big deal that he's flown me across the country to one of the most romantic cities in the world just so he can have me all to himself.

"Ready?" Jameson asks.

I blink. Am I ready?

"To go upstairs, Duchess?"

I wonder how long he's been trying to get my attention.

"Yes," I squeak, my nerves showing through the thin layer of calm I'm clinging to.

"If you need anything at all, please don't hesitate to let me know," the hotel manager interjects before we can exit.

"We will, Mr. White," Jameson reassures him. His hand settles over the small of my back, directing me toward the elevators. As soon as we're a few feet away his voice lowers, "I didn't think we were going to get rid of him. I thought our early arrival might allow us to delay that formality. Hotel managers always think they need to greet the boss."

"It's fine," I say while absently chewing on my lip.

Jameson studies me as we step through the gold, sliding doors into the mirrored elevator. "Don't worry, Duchess. I'll get you into bed."

Bed. There's that word again. My stomach drops out as the elevator begins to ascend. Each button lights up, taking us from the one marked L past the single digits then the double toward the very last button emblazoned with a PH. When we reach it, Jameson extends his arm. "After you."

We step into something that looks more like a foyer than a hotel corridor. Other than the emergency exit and a service lift there's only one marked door on this level.

Penthouse.

Jameson opens the door, but I look around in confusion.

"What did you do with Maddox?" I ask when I spot our bags waiting for us in the entry.

"I told him I could handle you from here." I don't miss the double entendre in his words.

"Would you like to freshen up?" Jameson asks after he locks the door behind us. "Or maybe I could draw you a bath?"

"No!" I practically shout but recover quickly. "Maybe just a quick shower."

Jameson's lips twitch, but he nods. "Follow me."

He doesn't bother to give me the grand tour. It's pretty

easy to make out the dining room table from the living room couch. That said, the space is huge and framed by large glass doors that overlook the city. Past them a small patio leads to a balcony. I can't help but shiver. I've had enough rooftop patios and plate glass for the summer. Thank you very much.

We pass through a corridor with several closed doors.

"What's behind those?" I point to them like a game show host.

"Other bedrooms," he says nonchalantly.

More than one bedroom? It's my understanding that most New Yorkers live in something roughly the size of a shoe box. We have a whole house at our disposal. This much extra space feels a bit like an insult.

"This is the master bedroom," he says, drawing me away from my thoughts.

I dare a peek at the king-sized bed that commands the center of the room.

"Maybe you should rest," he suggests, mistaking my interest in it.

I shake my head. I'm tired, but there's no way I'm about to fall asleep. He doesn't argue with me. Maybe he feels the tension, too. Instead he opens the door to the ensuite bathroom.

"You should have everything you need in here," he assures me before stepping away. "I'll give you some privacy."

Privacy isn't something I usually want from Jameson, but right now I'm glad to have it.

The bathroom is nearly as big as the bedroom and decorated in warm shades of white. I'm pretty certain we could fit a cocktail party's worth of people in the Jacuzzi. Actually, I could probably open my own spa here.

I opt for the walk-in shower, turning the water on to the sear setting. I can barely get my clothes off because I'm shaking so hard. Rummaging through the drawers of the vanity I find toothpaste, a razor, and a few other necessities like lip gloss and a hair tie. I also discover the handful of cosmetic items I occasionally use. Jameson didn't miss any details.

The steam from the shower rolls through the space, misting over the mirror. Shower's ready. I step under the cascade and hope the heat will clear my thoughts. But this isn't a sinus infection. This is sex, and my head is a muddled mess. I decide to go through the motions. I wash my hair and shave my legs. Then I just stand there and allow the water to flow over me as if I'm cleansing myself for some type of ceremonial offering.

"This is not your first time, Emma," I remind myself. But really it may as well be. I don't remember being nervous when I lost my virginity. Then again I didn't remember all that much about that night.

This is different. I want Jameson. I've wanted him since the first night we met. I'd stuck to my guns then, not allowing him entrance into my treasure chest. I'd promised myself I'd be in love before I had sex again, and I've been in love with Jameson for months. Now as summer days drifted away, I should be jumping into bed while I had the chance.

We'd had other opportunities this summer and there'd been no nerves in the heat of the moment. Jameson had been the one to stick to his rule about waiting until I was eighteen. Most of the time I'd been embarrassingly ready to go. The spontaneous horniness that accompanied a good make-out session had served as some sort of readiness lubricant. There'd been no room for over-analysis in my hormone-riddled brain.

"There's only one thing for it," I decide. "Close your eyes and think of England."

I shut off the water and realize my fingers look like raisins. "Super hot."

I vacillate between pumping myself up and tearing myself down as I towel off. Now comes the hard part: do I wrap myself in this or opt for my birthday suit? My eyes land on the solution to my problem: a silky robe hanging from a hook on the back of the door. I have no doubt it's been placed here especially for me. How long had Jameson been planning this little impromptu getaway?

Slipping it on, I knot the sash tightly as if girding my loins. Steam escapes into the empty bedroom. I half expected to find Jameson waiting for me here. Tiptoeing through the suite, I spot him on the patio outside. The first ribbons of dawn are creeping along the horizon, casting citrus hues over the buildings surrounding the hotel. With each passing second, the noises from the street below grow louder as the city begins its day.

So much for avoiding the roof top, I think to myself as I head toward him. Jameson doesn't turn as I step onto the patio behind him. When I reach him, I place my hand over his on the balcony.

"Did you find everything you needed?" His voice is thick with emotion. When he finally faces me, his gray eyes blaze with a ferocity I've never seen before.

I nod. I have now. I'm not the only who's worked up over finally going to bed together. Maybe he's not nervous, but it's as important to him as it is to me. It's all I really need to know.

"Jameson, I'm ready," I say in a soft voice.

He doesn't ask me to explain. Instead he sweeps me into his arms and carries me inside. The bed welcomes me as Jameson lays me across it. He takes a seat on the edge of the bed and reaches for his top button.

"Let me," I stop him. My fingers tremble as I undo each one until I'm shaking so hard that I fumble. His hands close over mine and he takes over the job until the button-down falls open. He shrugs it off and I reach for the flat panel of his chest, running my palm along the carved ridges of his pecs. I pause there feeling his heart beating under my hand.

Jameson's eyes find mine and I see the unspoken question in them. Can I feel the connection? The thread binding me to him? With my free hand, I untie the sash of my robe and allow it to fall. It's as good an answer as I can manage.

There aren't words to describe the feeling that's overcome me. He seems to understand this, and he moves beside me, drawing my body close to his. Brushing the wet hair from my face, he kisses each cheek, then my forehead, then along my jawline. He worships me slowly and my body softens under his touch.

Still after all this time, I'd expected a little more urgency. Jameson seems to understand the need to take it slow. We've been through a lot recently.

But my paranoia gets the best of me. Am I just laying here like some cold, dead fish? I reach up and tangle my fingers through his hair, tugging his face closer so that I can capture his lips. He surrenders, but only long enough to steal my breath away.

"There's no need to rush," he murmurs the reassurance.

I let him take charge then. There will be plenty of time for the more female-empowering positions of the Kama Sutra later. Right now, I give him my faith, my body, my everything.

He accepts it with each sweep of his mouth over mine and each caress of his hands on my body. I give myself to him, and he offers himself to me. We take and we give, allowing the heat of our bodies to conquer any apprehension we might feel. When my fingers find the buckle of his pants, his hands close over my wrist.

"Are you sure?" he asks.

I can't find the words, not with all the emotions swelling inside of me, so I nod. This simple act of consent speeds us along a bit, and my heels shove his pants down.

He settles against me and I can feel the heat of him. Even with our bodies still separate, in so many ways, we're closer that we've ever been before. We pause on the cusp of something that might change our relationship forever.

"I love you." His words are a vow. He traces them along the soft, bare contours of my body.

I find my voice, so I can repeat the precious statement. Three simple words that carry more weight than any others in the world.

Our lips crash together, his tongue flicking my mouth open so that he can deepen the kiss. I arch against him, but he doesn't accept the invitation. Instead, he breaks away, panting. Brushing his thumb over my lower lip, he smiles. "Hold on a sec, Duchess."

When he breaks contact, I bite my lip where he touched it, trying to resist the impulse to squirm. He tears open a foil packet. For a split second, I realize there's a lot of things we haven't discussed, and I make a mental note that it's time for me to get on the pill. Before I can berate myself for not being more cautious, he lowers his body over mine and the worries melt away.

I wiggle my hips, and he grabs them, holding me steady. His patience can be infuriating, but when I finally feel the first, hard edge of pressure, I gasp. My hands seek the sheets, and I grip them tightly.

A look of concern settles over his face. "Do you want me to stop?"

I shake my head. I guess my one and done experience a few years ago didn't qualify me as broken in. "I'm okay."

He moves slowly, gradually closing the last bit of distance between us and pausing occasionally to allow me to adjust. Once we've managed it, we stay like that for a few moments. Finally, I release my grip on the sheets, and hook my arms around him to signal that I'm ready. Jameson brushes his lips over mine, allowing the kiss to become something more organic. Our bodies take the hint, moving in rhythm with one another, until the slight discomfort I feel morphs into a small ripple of pleasure. Jameson responds to my pleased gasp with gentle urgency, rocking against me, and coaxing me towards my shattering moment of bliss. He meets me there with a low growl that tears through him.

Neither of us move for a moment. It took us so long to get here that the idea of breaking up the party now is unthinkable. Instead, our limbs twine together and we shift until we're on our sides, never breaking contact.

I've never really been one for long walks on the beach or love letters. But staring into the eyes of the guy you love after making love is pretty all right.

"What are you thinking?" he asks softly.

"That it was worth the wait," I confess, not bothering to hide a sheepish grin.

"And?" he presses.

"That I hope you're not going to make me wait that long for the next time," I tease.

He presses his forehead against mine. Our skin is damp with sweat, but he laughs. "How about we do it again right now?"

Wе fall asleep, tangled together, as dawn bursts into view outside our windows. When I blink dreamily a few hours later, the orange glow of sunrise has been replaced by late morning sunlight. I'm alone in the bed, so I roll over and stare at the ceiling.

Everything has changed and nothing has changed.

Except that I'm in a better mood then I can remember having been in for weeks. I giggle as I draw the sheet over my body. Then I yank it off the bed.

Tucking it around myself, I go exploring. When I reach the living room, Jameson grins at me over a cup of coffee.

"I thought you might be hungry." He gestures to the dining room table. It's been laden with silver platters and pitchers. I take the lid off a plate and then another.

"Did you order everything on the menu?" I ask.

"I thought the Duchess might have an appetite this morning," he teases.

I shove a piece of bacon in my mouth "The Duchess does."

I could stay like this forever, but I am in New York City.

"What are our plans today?" I ask as I pluck a promising looking croissant from a platter of pastries.

"I thought we could go out and see the city."

"Or we could stay in?" I suggest mischievously, my carnal side getting the better of me. "Neither of us are dressed after all."

Jameson abandons his coffee and prowls toward me, "What are you suggesting Miss Southerly?"

There's no resistance from me when he throws me over his shoulder and carries me back to bed.

It's nearly noon by the time either of us manage to get dressed. Jameson suggests another round of room service but I shake my head. "We'll never leave this suite if we do that."

"Tired of me already?" he asks.

"Never," I promise. I don't have to say more, he understands.

I've never been to New York and while I know the laundry list of tourist spots that I'm supposed to see, I defer to his wisdom.

We barely make it into the lobby before Mr. White accosts us.

"Mr. West, I was wondering if I might have a word with you?" he begins, but Jameson cuts him off.

"It's Saturday, Mr. White," he reminds him, "and I need to show my girl the town."

My girl, I think to myself. Everything sounds a little sexier coming out of his mouth this morning. Then again he'd given me a few demonstrations last night that showed just how sexy that mouth could be.

"Of course, of course!" Mr. White steps away and waves cheerfully, "Have a lovely day!"

"Unbelievable," Jameson mutters through clenched teeth.

"Give him a break." I can't help feeling benevolent today.

"If it was up to that man, I'd spend the entire weekend with his lips attached to my ass."

"No you wouldn't, I'd fight him for you," I promise.

"Oh yes?" he asks with a raised eyebrow.

"Definitely, that ass is mine."

I'm surprised when the car heads north. "Are we going away from the city?"

"Greenwich," he confirms. "I need to feed you. It's my responsibility after draining you of all your strength."

He takes me to a falafel place that's so small there's only room for a few bar stools at the counter. A charming mish-mash of colors compliments the simple menu of three items. Having never ordered falafel nor eaten it, I allow him to order for me. When he presents me with my food in a paper basket, I study it first.

"Trust me," he urges. I narrow my eyes but pick it the pita.

"What's in it?" I ask.

"Heaven," he says with a full mouth.

I take a bite and a variety of exotic, unrecognizable spices explode on my tongue. Next to me Jameson watches, clearly on edge, as I finish chewing and swallow.

"You know how you have all that money?" I ask. His face falls, no doubt he expects me to admonish him for not taking me to a fancy restaurant instead of this hole in the wall. "Can you buy one of these and put it in Belle Mère?"

"Your wish is my command, Duchess."

When we're finished, I'm stuffed. I can spy our car and driver, idling around the corner, but I stop Jameson before he can beckon it to us.

"Let's walk for a second," I suggest. I need to move if I'm going to digest this food baby I'm packing.

Greenwich, as it turns out, is charming. We find a row of brownstones lined by a canopy of trees. The emerald shade of their leaves makes it a few degrees cooler as we wander along. I sigh, my arm looped through Jameson's.

"Like it here?" he asks.

"So far I've only seen a king-sized bed and a falafel joint, and it's already my favorite place in the world. I might be biased though." Resting my head on his shoulder, I wonder how many times he's been here before. Maybe New York isn't as charming the hundredth time you visit, but it will always hold a special place in my heart. Jameson has been to cities all over the world. Do they hold a candle to this? "What is your favorite city?"

He flashes me a crooked grin that makes my knees weaken. "The one you're in."

"Charm will get you everywhere with me." I push onto my toes and kiss his cheek.

"Noted." He points to a brownstone with red lacquered steps leading to the front door. "That one."

"What about it?" I ask.

"It's for sale."

"What are we going to do with a place in New York? Especially when you own an entire hotel?" I ask. I'm guessing there might be a few other real estate holdings in the West family's New York portfolio. "Are you planning on leaving me any time soon?"

"Not if I can help it."

"Because I still have a year of prep left." I don't want the fairytale to end, but summer is fading around us. Soon we'll have to face the reality of our responsibilities in Belle Mère.

"And then what?" he asks.

"And then…" My mother had mentioned college before, but I'd always planned on sticking around and bailing Dad out of whatever new mess he found himself in at Pawnography. I never thought I'd get out of town. Las Vegas is a fly strip that's hard to break free from, but now it seems possible. So, where does that leave me? "I don't know."

"We'll figure it out," he promises me. "Maybe we can go on some college visits this fall. NYU. You'd probably love Boston."

"I'm not certain I have Harvard grades."

"You have Harvard money," he reminds me.

"What about you?" I interject, not wanting to consider if Hans's blood money could be used for that expense. "Don't you want to finish your degree?"

Jameson had left school—and the prescribed life his father had planned for him. Now that there is no one around to hold him to a vision of the future he didn't share, he has decisions to make as well.

"Most people go to undergrad and business school in the hopes that they'll land themselves at a fortune five hundred company," he says. "I'm already acting CEO of one."

No shit, Sherlock.

"But do you want it?" I ask in a small voice.

"I don't think it's forever," he admits. "In a few years, Monroe will be able to take over. I know she's always wanted to. My Dad was too stupid to realize she was the better choice for heir to the throne."

I gulp and look away before he can catch the suspicion I suspect is written across my face. Monroe has plans of her own but it's not my place to tell him about them. "What if it all crashed and burned?"

"Crashed and burned?" he repeats. "Are you plotting arson?"

"No need to call the lawyers." Or the nice men with

the strait jackets. "What if you just gave it up? You let it all fall apart? Without a West at the helm, what would happen?"

"Someone else would take over. There would be no crashing or burning. My family is invested enough within the company that we wouldn't even notice."

"Then why did you take over?" After the murder, Jameson had stepped up to take his father's place. I'd assumed the move was made out of necessity, since he hadn't wanted to inherit his father's position. But if what he's saying is true, then he did it for another reason.

"People needed reassurances," he explains. "My family, my mother, my sister. The people who work for our company. It's easier to accept the next person in line than to survive a power struggle within. If I play my cards right, I'll be able to step away when I'm ready and hand it over to someone else. It's figuring out how everything works and who everyone is first."

I don't have the smallest comprehension of what he's talking about. My family business employs one person and relies on the slave labor of its owner and daughter to survive. But I am relieved that he isn't stuck with West Enterprises forever. How long could he play the role of Nathaniel West before he became his father?

Jameson not too subtly shifts the topic of conversation from the serious turn it's taken to what I want to do this afternoon. That far ahead I can commit to. He suggests everything from a visit to the iconic Tiffany to a Broadway show, but I already know my answer. "Central Park."

"Central Park?" he repeats in disbelief.

"Horse-drawn carriage rides, mimes, there's a zoo."

"I thought you hadn't been here before," he says in an amused voice.

"I haven't, which is why I need to see Central Park." No amount of persuasion can sway me from this plan of action.

By the time we circle the block and find ourselves in front of the falafel shop once again, he's given up.

"This time of day it is going to be murder to get there," he grumbles as we climb into the back of the Lincoln.

I trail my finger down his thigh and blow him a kiss. "I have a few ideas on how we can pass the time."

AT ONE OF the many entrances to the park, there is a man who has painted himself entirely in white—his clothing to his face and his hands. I can't tear my eyes away from him. Apparently, this living statue gig is par for the course in Central Park, because Jameson is unimpressed.

"Take my picture!" I plant myself next to the man, who still doesn't move. Jameson groans and digs a few dollars out of his pocket. It's only then that I realize that this living art show is less about art and more about making money.

Regardless, I have mad respect for anyone who will brave body paint in this humidity.

After we get our shot, Jameson reluctantly agrees to allow me to eat a hot dog from a cart.

"How can you be hungry?" he asks.

"I'm battling an increased appetite. I feel like I ran a marathon this morning." Sex has to be good for the metabolism.

"Hopefully, that appetite doesn't lead to food poisoning." He ignores the dirty look the vendor shoots him from behind the cart.

As we meander through the twisting lanes of New York's most famous green space, I can't help becoming enchanted.

"I think I could be a New Yorker," I announce.

"That's a tall order," Jameson warns me.

"You don't think I could hack it? I grew up on the strip," I remind him as I toss the hot dog wrapper in a nearby trash can.

"You grew up in Belle Mère," he corrects me.

"And survived," I point out.

"Then you could probably make it anywhere," he agrees. Somehow we manage to miss the zoo. Instead, we happen upon a small pond surrounded by a low brick wall and a restaurant on one side. Little kids watch toy boats drift along its surface as their moms visit nearby.

"Most of New York is not this idyllic," Jameson tells me, but it doesn't matter.

Today of all days he can't scar my perfect vision of the world.

We find a spot under a nearby tree. Before I can claim the empty bench, I realize Jameson isn't beside me any longer. Whipping around to look for him, I find him the last place I'd expect.

"What are you doing down there?" I ask in a strangled voice. I can't help hoping that he's had a sudden onset of early arthritis to explain why he hasn't dropped to the ground like a normal person. Because he's not sitting on the grass. Instead, he is perched on one knee.

It takes a few seconds for me to process what's happening. When I finally do, I'm left with a choice but not the one he's given me. I opt to join him on the ground. Screw tradition. I need for us to be on an equal footing.

Dropping to my knees, I come face-to-face with the velvet box waiting in his palm.

"You don't have to do this," I whisper. "We're going to make it through this."

"That's exactly why I'm asking." Sincerity shines in his eyes. "Because we're going to get through this, and we'll get through whatever life throws at us next."

"Jameson, I can't—"

"Because you're too young?" he guesses. "You don't have to earn love. It's not a rite of passage. My love is yours. My everything is yours. That's not going to change."

"How can you be certain?"

"Are you certain?" he asks, turning the tide against me.

I don't hesitate. There's nothing to consider, because I know my answer to that question. "Yes."

"And I'm certain about this." Jameson flips open the box, forcing me to face the crossroads we've come to. "Will you marry me?"

I don't even have to think. My answer is already on my tongue. "Have you lost your mind?"

Jameson blinks. He wasn't expecting that answer. To be fair, I'm not entirely certain I meant to say it. I clap a hand over my mouth before it can get me in more trouble.

"No, I haven't lost my mind," he says in a flat tone.

"Then why?" I ask. "Are you still worried about being forced to testify against me? Because I think we've cleared that problem up. The FBI isn't—"

"This has nothing to do with that. That's our past. I'm focused on our future, Duchess."

"Does our future have to include the words 'till death do us part'?"

"Not if you don't want it to," he says fiercely. He snaps the box shut.

Crap. What have I gotten myself into this time? I grab it from his hands before he can shove it back into his pocket or toss it into the pond. There's no telling what he'll do.

Thinking quickly, I come up with a much more reasonable response. "I need to think about it."

The scowl darkening his face lightens.

"That's not a yes," I remind him.

"It's not a no, either," he says, interpreting my non-answer in his favor.

He leans closer, nuzzling my neck until I'm practically putty in his hands. "Is there anything I can do to persuade you?"

"Yes," I say, shoving him away. "Let me think about it. Also, maybe let me take a nap."

Between two lunches, a few broken hours of sleep, and

the emotional whirlwind he's just unleashed on me, being unconscious sounds pretty good. In fact, that my reaction to his proposal is to retreat or fall asleep should say a lot to him about my overall readiness for something as important as marriage. By agreeing to consider, though, I've rescued our weekend holiday.

Despite that, conversation is at an all-time low in the car. When we step back into the West New York's lobby, I'm relieved to see Mr. White waiting for us. I'm not certain he's ever moved.

Jameson lifts my hand to his lips and kisses it.

"Why don't you get some rest," he suggests. Before I can escape, he takes out the ring box that I'd given back to him in the car. He thrusts it into my hands. Apparently, we're going to play hot potato with it. "To help you think."

He winks before he turns to the over-eager White.

How can something so tiny feel so heavy? I wonder as I head up to the penthouse.

Maddox is waiting in the corridor. He unlocks the door for me, and I flush when his eyes linger on the ring in my hands.

So naturally I act like an adult and hide it behind my back.

"Did you have a good afternoon?" he asks. I don't miss the insinuation in his voice.

"It was interesting." I leave it at that, resisting the urge to treat him like a therapist and seek sanctuary in the suite instead. Heading straight for the bedroom, I deposit the box onto the dresser. But when I climb into the bed, it looks as if it's hovering above me. Scrambling up, I grab the box and put it on the nightstand. Then I turn over and squeeze my eyes closed. It's no use. I know it's there.

I had been too caught up in the insanity of the moment to even check it out before.

"You promised to think about it," I remind myself out loud. Rolling over, I pick the box up and open the lid. It's a whole lot of flawless. I'd seen enough diamond rings pass through the Pawnography showcase to know this one is worth a small fortune. I try not to think about that fact. If I had been the type of girl who dressed up as a princess or cried during romantic comedies, I might have pictured what my own engagement ring would look like. The truth is that the thought has never crossed my mind.

Now I know it could only ever be this ring. The square diamond in the center sparkles with a fiery brilliance that even I can't ignore. Smaller diamonds circle its edge and adorn the band.

I pluck it out of the box, and I'm surprised that something so sparkling and delicate could be so solid. I study it more closely and that's when I notice the inscription: To my leap of faith.

"I'm not crying. You're crying," I announce to the empty room. Hesitantly, I hold it over the tip of my ring finger as I blink back the moisture pooling in my eyes. It's too much change, too soon. But would it hurt to try it on?

Before I can decide, I hear Jameson enter the suite. Shoving the ring back in the box, I abandon it on the nightstand and nearly jump out of my skin when Jameson appears in the doorway.

"I didn't mean to scare you, Duchess."

Too late, I think, glancing at the box on the table next to me.

"I thought you were going to take a nap." His eyes stray to where his engagement ring sits unworn.

"I'm having a hard time turning my mind off."

"I can help you with that." He saunters, forward tugging his t-shirt over his head. The site of his perfectly stacked abs does a lot to relieve my anxiety. "Of course, maybe I don't want to take your mind off things."

He plays with the button on his jean, and I can't help licking my lips. "Maybe you could work on persuading me."

I don't bother to tell him that right now a few blissful moments of oblivion are exactly what I need.

"I can do that." He lets his jeans fall to the floor before he pounces onto the bed. "Allow me to show you one of the many benefits of marrying me, Duchess."

The next morning, the siren song of New York lures me out of bed. I leave Jameson sleeping peacefully, eager to venture out on my own. It's liberating to be in a city hundreds of miles from where you live especially given my newfound infamy in my hometown. Tugging my hair into a messy knot at the top of my head, I slip into a sun dress and sandals. I barely remember to grab my sunglasses before I head out the door. The hotel is quiet. In a few hours, the halls will be filled with people checking in and out, businessmen meeting for lunch, and the cleaning staff coming to make beds. I prefer it this way. I enjoy the relative anonymity of the crowds bustling along the street and the sense of being lost in the chaos.

It's nearly impossible to go unnoticed here, not when you're walking down the halls with Jameson West. It's a bit like being caught with the commanding general. The staff doesn't salute him, but everyone stops what they're doing and grovel. He's accustomed to it having spent his whole life bouncing around between his father's properties, shaking hands, and glad-handing; it's second nature to him. I prefer to blend into the wallpaper. The elevator delivers me to the first floor. I'm a few steps toward the staircase that will deposit me into the main lobby when I spot Mr. White; so much for going unnoticed. While the manager's effusive hospitality is understandable, I'm not up for it at seven in the morning.

I freeze at the top landing and begin to pivot slowly. If I take the elevator another flight down, I could exit through the bellhops' entrance; but before I can flee, Mr. White calls my name. "Miss Southerly. Miss Southerly." I do what any confident, well-adjusted woman would do in this situation. I pretend I don't hear him. Scurrying back toward the elevator, I jabbed the button and pray the cars haven't been called to higher floors. A light ding over my head, and I'm relieved when one opens just as Mr. White's insistent call grows closer. Inside, I press the button to close the doors and head to the lower lobby. It's empty, save for a bellhop who's too busy tagging stored luggage to notice me.

I push the sunglasses onto the bridge of my nose and head out the side door. Despite the early hour, it's already muggy. My forehead instantly dampens in the presence of the unfamiliar humidity. Growing up in Las Vegas I'm no stranger to heat, but desert heat isn't like this. By the time I happen upon a little pastry shop a few blocks away, I'm swiping at the sweat collecting under the rim of my sunglasses. I can't help but wonder as I stare into the pastry case if New Yorkers know how good they have it. Sure, back home I could choose between a gourmet champagne brunch courtesy of whatever celebrity chef has plastered his name on the local hotel or a massive buffet at all hours. There's no such thing as quaint in Las Vegas which means there's nothing like this there.

I order a bagful of French pastries that I can't pronounce and cappuccino. At least growing up in the desert has taught me how to drink hot coffee regardless of the temperature. I take my time heading back and watch as New York City comes to life, store fronts open, cars begin to clog the streets, and swarms of people descend on to the financial district to start the day. I try to maintain a leisurely pace but soon find myself swept along, forced to keep up with the current rushing about me. By the time I spot the familiar W emblazoned on the West New York Tower, I've finished my cappuccino and I'm ready for a cold shower. Zigzagging through the crowds toward the front entrance, I don't notice anything unusual until my feet hit the small courtyard outside the door.

Instantly, the air fills with shouted questions and camera clicks.

Click, click.

"Ms. Southerly, why are you in New York?"

Click, click, click.

"Can you confirm that you eloped with Jameson West?"

Click, click, click.

"What do you think about the allegations against your stepfather?"

Click, click, click.

"Is it true that you're pregnant with Jameson West's baby?"

I stumble forward, trying to worm my way past them. Somewhere along the line, I lose the bag of pastry. If the paparazzi think they're getting a photo op when I just lost my éclairs, they've got another thing coming. They crush forward hiding behind the cameras that they push into my face. I'm seriously considering going all Baldwin on them when a firm hand closes over my elbow.

I'm relieved to see Maddox standing in front of me. He pulls me through the crowd and whether it's due to the sheer size of him, or the unmistakable fury rolling off his body, the crowd of reporters parts like the Red Sea before us. Security guards are stationed at each door, providing a flesh and blood barrier to any journalists intrepid enough to try to get inside the West New York.

Jameson is at the front desk barking orders in a low voice to a trembling Mr. White, who looks even paler than his name suggests. Thankfully, the other hotel guests accustomed to five star establishments, and their celebrity clientele, discreetly look past us as Maddox delivers me to his boss.

"What were you doing?" Jameson turns his wrath on me.

I give him a blank stare.

"What were you doing out there?" he repeats.

Apparently, he's not getting the message. "I'm not on your payroll, Jameson West, so don't talk to me like I'm one of your ass-kissing employees."

Mr. White shrinks back behind the desk either afraid that this argument is about to go nuclear or seizing the opportunity to detach himself before Jameson can continue berating him.

"Mr. White says he tried to stop you." Jameson jerks his head at the manager, but he's no longer standing there. My boyfriend looks around for a moment before he gives up. "He says you ran off."

"That might have happened." I admit feeling a trifle sheepish for fleeing the premises earlier.

"Why would you do that?"

"Hold on." I cut him off. "I thought he was going to ask me how the room was and if we needed anything and give me those overeager puppy-dog eyes."

"No one stopped you on your way out?" Jameson asks. "There were no reporters?"

"I went out through the bellhops' entrance. It seemed like a good idea."

Jameson rubs his temples and his shoulders slowly slump into a normal position. "It was a good idea, Duchess. I'm sorry I yelled. When Mr. White called up to the room he was frantic, and to make matters worse, you weren't answering your phone."

I fish it out of my pocket and see several missed calls on its blank screen. "I didn't hear it ring."

He drops an arm around my shoulders and kisses my forehead. "It's okay, but we should probably go and pack."

"New York's been breached," I note with disdain.

"Two days of quiet are apparently the most we can hope for. Next time I'll take you to the Mediterranean. We have a private island in the south of France."

"Of course you do." I slip my arm around his waist as we wait for the elevator. But any semblance of normality is dashed by the hovering presence of Maddox. Although he stays a few feet away, he is impossible to ignore. "Is he going to follow us upstairs?"

"Yes, I think it's best that Maddox stays close by."

"Kinky," I whisper before sighing. "I had no idea the paparazzi was so virulent here."

"About that." Jameson tenses again, and I can feel the muscles in his back go rigid beneath my palm. "There have been some developments at home."

I move away from him. "What kind of developments?"

He doesn't answer. Instead he seizes my hand as we reach the top floor. Maddox arrives and takes up watch outside the door as Jameson leads us into the penthouse.

"What's going on?" I demand as soon as the door closes behind us.

"I already have my people on it," he says, but in no way reassures me.

Away from the crush of reporters screaming nonsensical questions at me, I start to recall what they were asking me. "Oh my God! They think ... and..."

"Maybe you should sit down," Jameson suggests. "I'll fill you in in a moment."

"Fill me in now."

"I will, but first I'm going to order you breakfast, Duchess."

"Oh, my pastries." I say, remembering how the bag fell underfoot, only to be trampled by the dozen people surrounding me. In the background, Jameson orders coffee and juice, eggs and bacon. I began to lose track. "Are we in this for the long haul?"

I wonder how long it will take to arrange for us to return home.

"The plane is on standby but there's no need to rush." Somehow I doubt that, but I keep this opinion to myself.

Whatever new scandal we've found ourselves embroiled in can wait.

"Can I see your phone?" he asks me. I hand it to him, not bothering to hide my suspicion. "What do you need it for?"

"You can have it back after your breakfast." He slides it into his pocket.

"What's going on, West?"

"Food first." He's not going to budge.

Room service arrives with lightning speed, one of the perks of being here with the owner. Jameson sits across from me sipping coffee and not speaking as I pile food onto my plate.

"Aren't you hungry?" I ask, between bites of eggs.

He shakes his head.

"I could have sworn you worked up an appetite last night."

He laughs, but his eyes remain distant. Swallowing my last bite, I slam the fork down on the table. "Out with it."

"It's on the cover of every major daily newspaper," he says in a steady voice.

"If you're trying to keep me calm, it's not working." My imagination has already kicked into overdrive. Do they have pictures of the proposal? Or, I gulp at the thought, something more personal. Maybe our late-night rendezvous on the patio last night was a bad idea.

"The FBI has arrested Hans on multiple counts of abuse, molestation, and child pornography."

The list of allegations especially the last one make my stomach flip over. *Child pornography*. If that's true, then he has pictures of Becca, and maybe even …

I don't finish the thought before I'm running for the bathroom. Jameson follows and kneels besides me as I wretch up breakfast.

"Maybe food was a bad idea," he says apologetically. "I thought it would be better if you ate before."

I shake my head to try to tell him this isn't his fault but the next round of vomiting sends another message. When everything is up, I sit on my heels and wipe my mouth. My knees shake as Jameson helps me to my feet. He oversees the appearance of a toothbrush and a glass of water.

"What else? I rasp out, my throat scratchy from vomiting.

"I'm having my people look into it, but otherwise it's the usual stuff."

"Usual stuff?" I raise an eyebrow. What's usual to Jameson West is prime tabloid fodder for the rest of us.

"It doesn't matter."

"I think it does." I plant my hands on my hips, refusing to follow him into the bedroom.

"The press got wind of us being here together and they might have jumped to conclusions."

"What kind of conclusions?" I ask slowly as I sort through the questions the paparazzi yelled at me.

"You've seen the cover of *Us Weekly*."

I have actually seen the cover of *Us Weekly*. My whole life I've been staring at it in the line at the grocery store or gas station. It's always plastered with news of celebrity divorces, marriages, births, and various scandals.

"Let me guess," I say, "not only did I murder your father, I'm also pregnant with your baby."

It takes me a second to realize that he isn't laughing because I'm actually right.

"Oh my God, are they saying I'm pregnant? We just had sex."

"I'll be sure to tell them that," he promises me dryly. "I don't think they're interested in the facts."

"Give me my phone." I hold out my hand.

"Duchess, I don't think that's a good idea."

"Give me my phone, West." He relinquishes it reluctantly.

"It's only rumors. We know that." I ignore him and

google my name along with his, only to discover a whole fresh crop of ridiculousness has been fed to the gossip rags in the last few days.

"They think we got married?" I shout as I scroll through. "Oh my God, does it look like I have a baby bump?" I run a hand over the plane of my abdomen as I stare at a photo that's headline news on TMZ.

"You do not have a baby bump. It's called Photoshop." Jameson gently pries the phone from my fingers before I can find the next horror story. "They've been running stories about us for months."

"Not like this." Conjecture has turned into rampant, imaginative bullshit. "I should call my mom, my dad, and I don't know, the *New York Times*? Somebody needs to set this record straight."

"I already have people working on it," he reassures me.

"Then why do we need to go home?" I ask after a long pause, "Let's go to the Mediterranean. Let's run away."

The truth is that the baby and wedding rumors are easy to face compared to what's going on with my stepfather. I can't bring myself to ask more about Hans. If I call my mother, will she want to talk about it?

"Wait," I say as realization dawns on me. "What do you know about the charges against Hans?"

If he already has people working on the fallout, it must be bad.

"We don't need to think about that right now."

"Now is a pretty good time. There's no food in my stomach. I'm less likely to throw up all over you."

"That's not it," he hedges. "I need confirmation before …"

"Before what?" My eyes narrow and I advance on him. If Jameson West thinks he's going to keep a secret from me right now, he's very much mistaken.

"I can't say this with absolute certainty," he says as I continue to corner him, "but the information we've gotten so far suggests your mother turned him into the FBI."

If Jameson thought this was going to upset me, he's wrong.

"She did?" I ask, awestruck.

"It's not confirmed, but it seems like it."

It hardly seems possible that I could ask so much. First, my dad showed up at the cemetery, remembering my birthday. Now, my mother has put aside her selfish fear of embarrassment and done the right thing.

"My parents are finally growing up," I whisper. I just had to show them how. Jameson doesn't respond. He simply wraps two strong arms around my shoulders and draws me close.

We stay like that for a long moment, gathering strength from one other. Then we walk out of this hotel. There will be more scandals to face, more questions, more scrutiny, but at least we'll face them together this time. It's a comforting thought.

Jameson's cell phone begins to buzz in his pocket. "Sorry, Duchess."

He kisses me quickly before he answers it. He remains silent so long that I begin to question if there's anyone on the other line. But I know from the way his face goes blank that he's listening.

"I understand. I can assure you that's not the case," he says in a clipped tone. "Of course, we'll see you soon."

"What was that about?" I ask as he pockets his phone.

"Time to pack. We've been called to a family meeting."

My dreams of joining the Mile-High Club are dashed by the perpetual influx of calls Jameson takes on the way back to Las Vegas. Considering the shock numbing my body, it's probably for the best.

The entire cabin of the West private jet has been turned into a miniature war room. The stack of newspapers waiting on the table when we boarded has been strewn across its entire surface. Each of the headlines is a glimpse into the situation awaiting us at home, and the picture it paints is bleak. Not only are the allegations against Hans as sickening as expected, but the reporters are doing an admirable job of tying all of the summer scandals into one big story.

Nathaniel West's murder has nothing to do with Hans van Essen but the fact that my former step-father had been planning to make a movie based on his death has encouraged journalists to jump to bizarre conclusions. The coincidence might have been left at that if it weren't for one common denominator between the two stories: me.

The milder features and editorials are in reputable newspapers. But the stack of gossip magazines delivered fresh from the presses take a bad situation and turn it into a nightmare. I'd been kidding when I joked earlier that the tabloids were reporting that I murdered Nathaniel West and was pregnant with Jameson's baby. Apparently, I have a knack for creative journalism, but the tales the tabloids spun of treachery and twisted family loyalties were beyond my scope of imagination.

Jameson takes another call and I sneak one of the gossip rags off the table and begin to read the cover story.

Summer arrived with murder in Belle Mère, Nevada, Las Vegas's most exclusive enclave. In a crime that shocked the nation, real estate mogul Nathaniel West was found murdered in his home atop the West Casino and Resort on the Las Vegas Strip. The discovery was made after his daughter, former reality star Monroe West, threw an end of the year party for her classmates at Belle Mère Prep.

The bizarre story doesn't end there. Initial investigation seemed to be directed at Nathaniel's son, heir to the West real estate empire. But what young billionaire is going to get his own hands dirty? Sources close to the investigation say that Emma Southerly, a friend of West's sister and a party-goer that fateful night, was so lovesick over Jameson that she agreed to carry out his plans for Nathaniel's murder.

What's in it for her? Newly released pictures have us speculating that she's providing Jameson West with more than an alibi. Is that a baby bump we spot? The two were seen canoodling in a New York eatery this weekend. According to a friend of Southerly, the couple was in New York to quietly elope. Has Emma Southerly seduced Jameson West or is this simply an attempt to secure their love child's future claim to the West fortune?

Regardless, Jameson West better watch his back where Ms. Southerly is concerned. According to a friend of the couple, the eighteen-year-old prep-school senior has major daddy issues and might have been one of her step-father, Hans van Essen's many victims.

If the two are looking for honeymoon suggestions, might we suggest a brief trip to couple's therapy?

I reach the end of the page and a strange emotion begins to bubble inside me. A few seconds later, I'm laughing. Jameson steps back into the main cabin, eying me with concern as he finishes his latest phone call.

"No one will believe that," he informs me, taking the magazine from my hands and dumping it ceremoniously into a nearby trashcan.

"People will believe it," I tell him. "They're always going to believe these things about me. I'm just a gold-digger desperate to get my claws into you, after all."

Jameson's jaw twitches. "If that's the case, I take it I finally have my answer."

It takes me a minute to realize he's referring to his proposal. The gossip rags might take away my dignity, but they won't take my freedom. I shake my head. "I'm not going to make life decisions based on tabloids. But you're right. I have made my decision."

"And?" he asks through gritted teeth.

"No," I tell him softly. He begins to turn away before I add, "And yes."

"That's not an answer, Duchess," he warns me in a cold voice.

"Let me clarify." I stand up just as we hit a pocket of turbulence, and I'm thrown forward. Jameson catches me. I half expect him not to, given the chilling distance he's demonstrating.

"Not right now. In five years, when I'm done with college, or my first parole has been granted"—at the rate we're going, either seems equally possible—"then yes, I will marry you...if you still want me."

"I will always want you." His promise takes my breath away. There's an absolute certainty to it that not even I can doubt.

"But I'm not marrying you to solidify an alibi or to legally prevent you from having to testify against me." I need to be clear in this, especially as we jump into the fray at home.

"I don't want you to marry me for those reasons. I want you to marry me because you love me," he says sharply. "I didn't ask you as a means of strategy. I asked you because you ran away and I thought I'd lost you. I never want to lose you again."

"You won't. But you don't have to put a ring on it to keep me from running away again."

"But you ran the first time," he reminds me. A note of accusation in his tone.

"I had a reason to then."

"There is never a reason to run from me, Duchess," he growls. I want to point out that he's completely wrong about that, or at least I thought he was. "Promise me you won't run again."

"I won't run again," I vow, starring up into his eyes. His arms tighten around my waist possessively.

"What does it matter if we get married young?"

"You aren't going to let this go, are you, West?" I push onto my tiptoes and give him a soft kiss.

"That wasn't an answer." Before we can continue to debate our relationship in philosophical terms, his phone rings again.

"Go on and take it," I urge him. "I'll still be here when you get back."

He hesitates long enough that the phone goes to voicemail.

"Just one thing." His arms fall away from me, and, a moment later, he retrieves something from his pocket.

"Technically you said yes, Duchess," he says as he pops open the ring box.

"Listen," I say, pulling away. "Your mom demanded we come home, probably because she wants to make sure we didn't go to New York to elope. I don't want to give her a heart attack."

"Believe me. My mother has endured far worse shocks

than this." He ignores my protest and slips the platinum band onto my ring finger.

"The tabloids are going to have a field day with this," I warn him.

"Let them." And for the first time today, a genuine grin brightens his handsome face. "I want the world to know you belong to me."

"Belong, huh? They think I'm a blood-thirsty, psychopathic gold-digger. I think the world assumes you belong to me."

His laughter dissipates the tension in the air. "Then they'll know you're my psychopathic gold-digger."

Monroe's nails click on the polished mahogany top of the dining room table. If being under the scrutiny on tabloid surveillance teams is awkward, this is unbearable.

"He'll be out in just a minute," I say apologetically for the tenth time. Later tonight I'm going to have to talk to Jameson about abandoning me to the mercy of his mother and sister in the middle of a crisis. Maybe it's unfair given that he's probably on the phone trying to handle the situation, but his absence only gives them more time to sharpen their claws.

Monroe runs her tongue along her teeth across the table from me.

She's going to eat you alive, a tiny voice warns me. Tell me something I don't know.

Evelyn, Jameson's mother, has been eerily silent since our arrival. Usually she's the warmest member of the family, having gone out of her way to make me feel welcome, despite the circumstances under which Jameson and I met. Tonight, she seems to have taken a page out of her son's book, keeping her thoughts and emotions under wraps.

She sits at the head of the table; her black silk blouse a stark contract against the creamy white of her throat. A string of pearls nestles against her collarbone. From all outward appearances, this woman is in mourning. Knowing what I know about the nature of the West family, her show of grief is less about actual sadness and more about propriety—a topic I have a feeling I'm about to get a lecture in.

"Mother. Monroe." Jameson greets his family as he strides into the dining room. It feels like ages since we've both been in his Mount Charleston home. Can it really only have been a few days? The boy who brought me here a few months ago has been replaced by a man in a white oxford and suit pants with his sleeves rolled up to the elbows and his tie unknotted at his neck. I miss the t-shirt and jeans. I miss the picnic basket with crunchy peanut butter sandwiches, but most of all I regret that he's given it all up to protect me.

Monroe clears her throat. "Can we get going with this? I have plans this evening."

I shoot her a look that suggests I suspect what those plans might be, but she maintains her studied indifference as she inspects her manicure.

"Of course we can—now that we're all here," Evelyn

West says in a benevolent tone. Jameson takes the seat at the opposite end of the table, and the tension between them is palpable. On one end, his mother still reeling from the murder of his father, has been left to parent two children who took the Autobahn into adulthood. On the other end sits her son, who has risen to power in the absence of his father. I'm glad I'm not battling for which end is up, but being stuck in the middle sucks.

"Well, you called this meeting," Jameson prompts.

"We're sorry to interrupt your little holiday in New York," Monroe sneers, "but you left a mess behind yourselves."

I grip the edge of the table, trying to maintain some sense of decorum. Considering that my relationship with Monroe has primarily consisted of flipping the bird to each other behind the backs of teachers for the last three years, this is harder than it sounds.

"Monroe." Her mother's voice is rich with admonishment. "I asked us all to be here because this concerns all of us."

"I don't see how what her stepfather did…"

I'm halfway out of my seat when Jameson cuts her off.

"Shut up, Monroe."

"You can't speak to me like that."

"I don't know why you think I can't," he growls.

"You will both be quiet." Evelyn's fist pounds the table. "Neither of your names have been dragged through the mud half so much as poor Emma's, and you don't see her starting fights."

I shrink further into my chair, thankful that she doesn't realize how close I'd been to lunging across the table for Monroe's throat. Jameson takes the heat for me, squaring his shoulders and meeting his mother's gaze with defiance.

"Is this a family meeting or a lecture?"

"It seems you are in need of both, my son." Their eyes stay locked on each other, providing Monroe and I with some common ground as we glance at them nervously.

I hadn't expected a play for power between the two of them, but then again, I never expected to find myself in this situation at all.

"I called this meeting to clarify some points of interest," his mother explains.

"Then why is she here?" Monroe asks.

"Because she is a part of this family," Jameson informs her tersely. Meanwhile, I twist the engagement ring he insists I wear around to hide the diamond, stealing a glance at my hands and my lap. I wonder if it would be better to change it to the other hand. There's something blatant about wearing it on this one.

"Is it true?" Monroe demands. "Is that why she's hiding that rock she showed up wearing? You can take it out from under the table. You aren't fooling anyone."

So much for that plan. Evelyn keeps her eyes trained on her son.

"Of course Emma is welcome as a member of this family. You've made your feelings about her quite clear, and while I can respect that, I would like to know if congratulations are in order."

I open my mouth, my cheeks turning a lovely shade of candy apple red, but Jameson beats me to the punch.

"Do you believe everything you read on the Internet, Mother?" he asks dismissively.

"No, I don't." She folds her hands in front of her. "But, as your sister pointed out, and as my accountants informed me, your girlfriend is wearing a stunning, million-dollar engagement ring."

"Holy shit," I blurt out. I'd expected the ring cost bank, but not the actually contents of a small bank.

"Don't get practical now, gold-digger," Monroe says.

"You will not call her that," her mother informs her as Jameson gets to his feet.

"None of this is any of your concern."

"On the contrary"—Evelyn gestures for him to sit back down—"given the concerns Agent Mackey and the FBI have presented to me, and the speculations of the media, it's very much my concern."

"I've already addressed those concerns," he says through gritted teeth.

"I'm not here to be part of a cover-up," Monroe interjects.

"Maybe I should go," I say nervously. The West family has enough to deal with without being overly concerned with my problems.

"Nonsense, this concerns you. I simply want to know if you two are married."

"No," I cry out, overwhelming Jameson's more calm denial. He might not care about what his mother thinks of me, but I do. "And we're not getting married."

"Is that a placeholder, then?" Monroe asks.

"I told him he has to wait. I'm not marrying him to get the FBI to back off, and I'm not not marrying him to avoid the scandal. I just told him that I would marry him in a couple of years if we still want to get married."

"That sounds very practical." Evelyn's lips twitch, but she keeps smile to herself. "I'm glad one of you is thinking clearly."

"I'm old enough to get married," Jameson reminds his mother.

"Yes," she admits, "but your girlfriend it not. I'm glad you finally found someone to ground you in reality. Lord knows, I've never been able to."

"Well, now that that's out of the way." Jameson's voice is cold, showing neither the embarrassment I feel or the amusement his mother is hiding. "We should be going."

"Don't be ridiculous. There are other matters to consider."

"I'm not pregnant," I jump in, wondering if she's concerned over that particular headline as well.

"I didn't think you were, given that Jameson and I had an understanding." She gives him a pointed look. "It would be quite miraculous if you were. Of course, now that you're eighteen, I would ask that you wait a few years before you make me a grandmother."

I flush. She knows exactly why he took me to New York.

"I think we need to discuss other situations, particularly the allegations your father is facing."

"Stepfather," I corrected her. Monroe rolls her eyes across the table. I don't care if it seems like a petty difference to her, it's a huge difference to me.

"Stepfather," Evelyn grants me. "I have a few questions."

I gulp, feeling a hard knot forming in my throat. "Of course."

"You don't have to talk about anything unless you want to, Duchess," Jameson calls from the other end of the table, but I hold up my hand.

"I want to. This is a family meeting after all, and apparently, I'm officially a West, married or not."

"Some of my questions are a trifle delicate," she warns me, and I nod. "First of all, our lawyers would like to talk with you when you have a moment about the film project your stepfather was involved with regarding my late husband."

"I'll tell them what I know about it," I promise, adding silently, *which isn't much.*

"Secondly, Monroe would like to say something." Evelyn turns her attention to her daughter.

"It's come to my attention that I allowed a snake to get too close to the family, and she's struck."

"Stop talking in riddles," Jameson demands.

"Sabine," Monroe clarifies. "Apparently, she was quite smitten with Levi. The two of them have been seeing each other behind my back for a couple of weeks."

"Christ, Monroe," Jameson mutters, running his hands through his hair. I don't need her to continue. I know exactly what this means. Sabine has always been Monroe's right-hand bitch, which means she knows more about the sordid affairs that go on behind the West family's closed doors than nearly anyone not sitting at this table.

"I apologize," Monroe continues, "and I'll be more judicious in my choice of friends in the future."

Judicious? It's more like she's taking the SAT's than apologizing, but I keep my mouth shut. Sabine might have seemed like a loyal lapdog; however, their friendship had always been based on fear and control. None of us should be surprised that she took the opportunity to stab Monroe in the back at the first opportunity. Judging from Monroe's detachment, she even seems a little proud.

"Now that that's settled." Evelyn swivels to face me. "I would like to know if the allegation that your stepfather molested you is true."

"Mother, that is none of your business," Jameson interrupts her.

"You've made your intentions towards Emma clear."

"So you want to embarrass her?" he asks.

She levels a stare that could probably melt iron at him. "Embarrass? Is that what you think of me? My support, financially and emotionally is entirely behind your girlfriend."

"Fiancée," he corrects her, and I wince.

"Let's let her get used to the idea," his mother suggests.

"I'm asking her, because if it's true, I'd like to arrange for her to see a therapist."

"I don't think," I begin.

"That's not your place," Jameson interjects.

"You'd like this woman to be my daughter," she points out to him, "so I'm treating her as I would my own daughter. If Monroe were in this situation, I would urge her to do the same."

I can't help but stare at Monroe. If Evelyn West had any idea what type of situation she's in, we'd be having a different conversation right now. Monroe's facade of disinterest slips, and I see the fear in her eyes. She knows I can burn her, and I have every reason to do so. Particularly, after learning how she's used Jonas for the last couple of years, but this is a family meeting, and if Evelyn West wants to treat me like a daughter, then I need to treat Monroe like a sister.

"I don't think it's necessary," I explain to Jameson's mother, "because he didn't molest me."

She releases a deep breath. Someday she'll learn the particulars—that Hans von Essen raped my sister—but, for now, she needn't know it was his actions towards me that brought him to his knees. No, Evelyn West doesn't have to worry about me. Hans von Essen didn't get the better of me.

I destroyed him.

Now that the emotional part is out of the way, she shifts into business mode. "Naturally our lawyers and publicity team have been following the events. They will be at your disposal should you need them when dealing with the authorities or with the press."

"Of course." I swallow hard at the thought. Is this what the rest of my life will be if I join this inimitable family? Family meetings and strategy sessions, all designed to dictate how the world sees us. It's overwhelming to consider.

"Jameson, might I have a minute with you alone?" his mother asks. The two of them step into the study across the hall, leaving Monroe and I to face one another.

"You didn't rat me out," she says.

"I thought it in poor taste, given ..." I trail away. I can't bring myself to say it.

"That you're a West now?" she finishes for me.

"I guess," I say with a shrug, hoping that I appear nonchalant, even as my heart speeds up.

"Why do you think I advised you to stay here this summer?" Monroe asks. "There's a lot you have to learn about this family."

I glance toward the study doors, which have been shut behind mother and son. "You're telling me."

"Just to clarify, we're not best friends or anything," Monroe says.

"Agreed. So long as you tell me you're not planning to sabotage me at the first opportunity."

"Do you think I wouldn't sabotage my friends?" She laughs, as though the suggestion of her loyalty is preposterous.

"Remember how you told me you needed to teach me

how to be a West?" I ask her. "I think maybe it's time for me to teach you how to be a decent human being."

"Too late for that, I'm not interested." If my barb stings, she doesn't show it. "But rest assured, you're better off being my family than my friend."

My eyebrow arches. "And why is that?"

"Because this family protects each other. *No matter what.*"

"So I'm one of you then?"

"You could have delivered me to my mother. You could have told her the truth about what you know. She'll find out eventually, of course. It's an inevitability in my plan, but it wouldn't have done you any good with her or with me. You've proved yourself to be a West with your loyalty."

"I'm not even sure what that means," I admit.

"It means you know how to keep a secret, and it means you'll protect us, *no matter what you know.*"

That I'm dating a real estate mogul's heir has never seemed more important than when Jameson unlocks the door to a penthouse suite in an off-the-strip property. The idea of going anywhere that people might recognize us makes me want to vomit and after tonight's awkward family meeting, I need a little distance from the rest of the Wests. If I'd thought that being labeled as a prime suspect in a murder trial was going to be my worst memory of summer vacation, I know now that I was wrong.

As if facing the impending storm of questions from my parents and friends isn't bad enough, Jameson hadn't said one word to me since we left Mount Charleston. Whatever his mother had spoken to him about in private hangs between us, dampening the mood.

"This is nice," I say conversationally, but he only shrugs. The resort he's brought us to is one of those luxury joints masquerading as a haven from the bright lights and business of Las Vegas. Judging from the info I'd skimmed while Jameson did his bit to shake hands and make nice with the management, it's a timeshare for gambling addicts that have the good sense to keep some mileage between their wallet and the craps table.

The suite is decorated in subdued hues of beige, perfect for whoever might call it home for a week at a time. It's more nondescript and a lot less stylish than the other West resorts I've seen, but the leather couch still shines with furniture polish and the pillows on the gigantic bed remain fluffed.

I eye it and realize that I have one weapon in this cold war we're silently battling. As I slip my sundress over my head, catching Jameson's attention, I realize how fortunate I am to be a female. The low back of my dress and its tiny straps made wearing a bra impossible. Yes, it's completely unfair to flaunt my body to get my boyfriend to talk to me, and some might argue I'm setting women back like a hundred years, but personally, I've never been so happy to have boobs.

"Not going to work, Duchess," he calls from the living room as I drop onto the bed.

Arranging myself artfully like the chick in Titanic, I respond. "I can't hear you. Come closer."

"I said you are infuriating," he growls as he steps into the bedroom. But the annoyance in his words can't mask the ways his eyes linger on me.

"What big eyes you have, Mr. West."

"I'm not playing around here." He grabs a robe from the back of the door and tosses it to me.

I shrug it on angrily. So much for my irresistible feminine wiles. "I'm not either, but I'll do what I have to if it means you'll talk to me."

"Why don't you try talking to me?" he suggests in a flat voice.

That hadn't occurred to me, but I'm not letting go of my bruised ego so easily. "I've been talking to you."

"Small talk about the decor isn't a hot conversation starter."

If he's trying to up the alert level of my fury, he's doing a damn good job.

"I don't want to fight with you," he says in a soft voice.

"Your mom is pissed, isn't she?" I guess. When he nods, I wish a sinkhole would form and swallow me alive.

"Not at you," he clarifies when he sees my expression.

"If she's mad at you, then it's because of me."

He doesn't bother to challenge that assumption. "I knew we would get flack for being engaged. This will pass."

"Maybe I shouldn't..." I twist the ring he's given me around until it reaches my knuckle but he strides over and pushes it back down my finger.

"That's your birthday present," he reminds me.

"It's a whole lot more than a birthday present." Staring at it, I wonder how such a little thing can mean so much. Then I remember the price tag and the disdainful look in Monroe's eyes when she called me a gold-digger. "I don't need a ring. I'm not really the jewelry type."

I fail to add that every girl I know is the diamond type even if they've never owned so much as a friendship bracelet before.

"Duchess, I want you to wear it." He leans over the bed and tilts my chin up with his finger. "It's important to me and since you won't marry me yet, let's call it a compromise."

I narrow my eyes at him. He's not fighting fair. How am I supposed to say no with those silvery-gray eyes gazing into mine? It's not even a discussion. "I thought we were calling it a present."

Jameson laughs, slipping his hands under the collar of my robe and gently shucking it free from my shoulders. I allow the sleeves to slide off my arms and the garment falls off, pooling behind me. His eyes stay glued to mine even as his jaw twitches. "I've been imagining that ring—and only that ring—on you since I bought it."

"And aren't you going to look?" I purr. I'm not entirely certain if I've won or lost this argument, but I can't seem to care.

His gaze sweeps over me, leaving goosebumps in its wake. I drape my arm over my bare hip and put his ring on display. He lingers on it and with each passing second, my pulse ratchets up in speed. Finally, I reach up and grip his shirt, urging him to join me on the bed. As I unbutton it, his face slants down, nuzzling into the curve of my neck.

"It's not just a present," he whispers.

My answer catches in my throat. "I know."

He pulls back and studies me for a moment. "You don't have to wear it."

I cup his face with my palm and smile shyly. "I think I want to. I just never expected to have something so..."

Extreme? Expensive? Unexpected? I can't find the right word.

"It's a ring fit for a duchess." But Jameson understands, taking my hand in his, he lays me across the bed. "For my Duchess."

Biting my lip, I marvel as his body moves against mine, slowly pushing all my doubts away.

THE NEXT MORNING I'm alone in bed, stretching my muscles. Is everyone this gloriously sore after sex? Or has Jameson West cornered the market on wearing a girl out? Either way, I'm not complaining. I find a note next to a fresh pot of coffee in the living quarters.

Dealing with fall-out. Call me when you're up.

Love,

Jamie

I take a risqué selfie instead. His response is immediate and I answer the phone as soon as it begins to vibrate.

"Thank god you're eighteen," he says gruffly.

"Why are you whispering?" I ask, unintentionally lowering my own voice.

"Because I'm in a boardroom with a bunch of middle-aged men who already drool over my fiancée. I don't need to give them any more material to fantasize about," he admits.

"Then you better delete that photo." I pour a cup of coffee and take a slow sip.

"That photo and I are going to have some alone time together later," he promises.

"How about you hold out for the real thing?"

"Just promise you'll stay like that the rest of the day and we have a deal." I can hear the wicked smile in his voice. "Duchess, I have to go. I love you."

"I love you, too." I hang up and look around the room. I'm not entirely sure how I'm not floating mid-air right now. Before I can come down from my high, my phone rings again and I answer it immediately.

"Yes, I am naked, but you're going to have to be patient."

"I'll keep that in mind," Agent Mackey says dryly. "I guess you didn't want to wait for your test results—or you didn't care."

My temper flares and I have to set my coffee mug down to avoid spilling it all over myself. I'm mad at myself more than her, but that doesn't mean she's getting a free pass. Not this time. "We had private testing done. Your lab didn't seem as concerned with the results as we were."

"Ah, the royal *we*. How is the pedestal he's placed you on?" she asks.

"Did you call for anything else?" I can barely get the words past my gritted teeth.

"Mostly to deliver the good news, but when you have a moment I'd like to get a statement from you regarding your stepfather."

I swallow against the bile rising in my throat. Mackey is never going to allow me to be happy. She'll always find a way to disrupt my life. "I have nothing to say about him."

"That's interesting. I'd still prefer we talked," she presses.

"You're never going to let this go, are you?"

"Let what go, Miss Southerly? Or are you Mrs. West now? It's hard to keep up with the gossip."

I bypass the jab and focus on the real issue. "You have your DNA results. You know it wasn't me. You know it's not Jameson. When are you going to stop this persecution?"

"Persecution is a strong word," she warns me. "As far as the FBI is concerned, you've been cleared. There's no evidence to substantiate your involvement."

"And as far as you're concerned?"

"I'll let it go when I know who's responsible for Nathaniel West's murder."

"It wasn't us!" I've completely lost my cool now.

"But it was. Maybe not you or Jameson, but it was one of you. Someone at that party killed Nathaniel West and whoever he or she is, they think they've gotten away with it. I'm here to make certain that you can't go on buying your way out of trouble. Don't fool yourself. A lot of people wanted him dead, and someone close to you saw that it happened. How well do you know your new family, Emma? How much will they pay to keep the truth locked away?"

"I've never bought my way out of trouble," I say flatly.

"No, but you sold your soul to a man who did."

WHAT JAMESON DOESN'T KNOW CAN'T hurt him, which is why I don't tell him I'm leaving the suite. I bribe Maddox to keep quiet with a venti white chocolate mocha, his guilty pleasure. I even allow him to drive me. Given the increased interest in my personal life, having a body guard the size of The Rock around seems like a good idea. Plus, it's pretty easy to feed Maddox bullshit.

"I need to run an errand for my dad," I say. "This guy brought a bogus baseball card into the shop the other day and I have to deliver the bad news that it's a fake."

Tucking a little kernel of truth into my lie makes it easier to sell. Don't say I never taught you anything.

Maddox pulls into a spot in front of Dominic Chamber's office and I jump out before he can unbuckle his seat belt.

"I'll only be a minute," I promise him. He looks unconvinced. Probably because I've pulled a few over on him. I take my phone out of my bag and drop the bag on the passenger seat. "Consider this collateral. I'll be right back."

Chambers puts out a cigarette as soon as I enter. "Sorry, about the smoke, Miss Southerly."

"Not going to ask if I've changed my name?" I ask dryly. He'll be the first person I've seen since my return to Las Vegas not to.

"Why would I ask that?" His bushy eyebrows knit into one woolly caterpillar over his eyes.

"Nothing. Rumors. Tabloids." I'm more than happy to not explain.

"Oh that." He waves a hand. "I never believe that crap."

I nod in agreement. Finally, a reasonable response.

"Plus, I checked wedding license applications in New York. I know you didn't get married," he adds.

"I think that's a breach of my privacy," I inform him.

"I am a private eye," he says as if that absolves him of his nosiness.

"Did you receive my advance?" I'd taken the liberty of PayPal-ing a significant sum through Chamber's website, hoping it would encourage him.

"I did. Much appreciated. I'm happy to report that I have something for you as well." He tosses a folder across his desk to me.

"Is this...?"

"Better than a few pictures, huh?" he says with pride.

I'd asked Dominic for a picture or a document that only the police would have. Instead he delivered the mother lode.

"Las Vegas PD is surprisingly easy to bribe," he continues. "Plus, I think they want to stick it to that FBI agent who thinks she's running the show."

"They aren't the only ones," I mutter. I skim through the contents of the Nathaniel West case file, glancing away when I reach the crime scene photos.

"He was a bastard, but he didn't deserve that," Chamber says thoughtfully.

"No, he didn't," I agree. Standing to leave, I assure him that the rest of the agreed upon fee will be arriving shortly. Before I reach the door, he stops me.

"If you don't mind my asking: what are you going to use it for?"

I flash the detective a coy smile. "Bait."

The West Resort and Casino has a lovely afternoon brunch even during weekdays, which is why I choose it for a bite to eat. Plus, it gives me a chance to put my invited guest in her discomfort zone. I need Monroe West if I'm going to use the information I've gotten from Dominic Chamber to my advantage. I'm already seated by the time she arrives, and my earliness makes me feel as if I have the upper hand.

Perhaps that's why my mother always gets to a restaurant thirty minutes in advance.

Monroe's annoyance radiates from her. While her lacy, navy dress and nude flats make her look the part of the innocent, I know exactly how I got her to meet me today. That's probably why her sharp blue eyes cast daggers at me from across the dining room.

"Did you have to call my agency?" Monroe hisses as she takes the seat across from me.

I shrug, stirring a packet of sugar into my tea. I'm not certain this is what people mean when they say kill them with sweetness. "It seemed the easiest way to reach you."

"You have my phone number." She orders a mimosa from the waiter and then turns her fury back on me.

"I forgot."

She considers this for a moment, and I hold my ground. Bullies respond to strength, so if I want to bond with my future sister-in-law, I'm going to have to show her exactly what I'm made of.

"So did you miss me or is there a point to this little afternoon tea party?" she asks, lounging into her seat. She's getting comfortable, which means she's letting me win this round.

Score one for Emma.

"I received some good news today. I've officially been cleared in your father's murder case."

"We've known that for a while, though."

I can't quite hide my surprise. I had no clue that Jameson had shared the DNA issue with the rest of his family.

"Don't look so shocked," she says. "We keep each other's secrets, remember? Although no wonder he was so upset. It would have been pretty fucking twisted if you were his half-sister."

Score one for Monroe.

"Of course, maybe that gets you off," she continues, smothering a roll with butter before proceeding to pick at it.

"You're more of the expert on fetish," I assure her as I take a sip from my straw.

I don't miss the slight flinch she tries to hide.

Score two for Emma.

"I thought we could celebrate," I begin.

"That you aren't screwing your brother? Sure, why not?" She rolls her eyes and abandons the uneaten roll on her plate.

"That I'm free and clear. Unless there's a reason we should be concerned about familial involvement." I don't hide the implication of my words. I'm calling Monroe's bluff. I'm not Nathaniel West's daughter, but she is.

"Don't be a pervert," she says flatly. "So you want to have a party."

I nod, trying not to look too self-satisfied that I've gotten her on the same page. "Here."

"Here?" Monroe repeats. "You mean upstairs? Is that a little tasteless?"

"I had no idea you were so concerned with other people's opinions. Maybe we should burn the place down and rebuild." Monroe doesn't seem to care that her father was murdered in this building. She's stayed here, conducted business here. Hell, she even threw another party here.

"My mother is concerned with saving face," she reminds me.

"This is about showing our strength," I counter, hoping that this fledgling family connection is strong enough to get this done. "To whoever is watching. We own this town and they aren't going to scare us away."

"You aren't a West yet. We might protect you but let's wait for the prenup before you go claiming to own my family's empire," she suggests drolly.

I slide my hand around my glass and lift it so that my engagement ring sparkles in the afternoon sunlight. "Oh honey, I already own it."

When I step off the escalators to the lobby, I'm met with half of the hotel's security team. So much for keeping a low profile. Maddox shrugs through the crowd of suits. We both know that when Jameson wants to make a scene he's going to.

"Miss Southerly, I've been asked to escort you upstairs." It's hard to take the man speaking to me seriously given that he's wearing sunglasses inside the building, but I do my best.

Following him toward the bank of elevators that lead to the business offices, I spot Jameson waiting for me. His tie is still knotted tightly at his throat and his suit is pressed. I'm used to seeing him later in the day when he's ditched the veneer of respectability. The man standing in front of me is far too respectable and it's having an undeniable effect on me.

He takes me by the hand, thanking the guard.

"I thought you were staying home," he whispers. "I

have to admit that I was rather enjoying visualizing you naked in bed, waiting for me."

"Are you disappointed to see me?" I ask, brushing a chaste kiss over his lips.

"Never," he promises, rubbing the stubble peppering his jaw. Without thinking, I reach up and run a finger along it.

"You need to shave," I murmur.

"I shaved this morning." His mouth closes over mine before I can continue to critique his appearance. Despite the tension coiling through my limbs, I melt against him. When we finally break apart, I gasp for breath. "Just think of it as friction, Duchess."

"I like it," I simper.

He doesn't mistake the double meaning and without a word, he grabs my hand and strides toward the elevator.

"Are you on a break?" I call, trying to fish my phone out of my bag with my free hand.

"No." He continues forward and to my surprise, he bypasses the private elevator and steps into one crowded with people. Jameson shifts behind me to make room for another passenger, giving him the opportunity to grab my hips and pull me against him. His dick presses against my butt and my breath hitches. Just imagining what's about to happen, tightens my stomach and when we step off the elevator a few floors later. I glance around.

"Where are the hotel rooms?" I ask in confusion, staring at a corridor of meeting rooms and banquet halls.

"If I take you near a bed, I won't get back to work

today, and"—he checks his phone— "I have a meeting in fifteen minutes."

"Don't let me keep you," I taunt him, letting my hips sway a bit as I walk.

"Not until you answer a question." He grabs me around the waist and holds me. Meanwhile I've stopped breathing. Jameson didn't spot me by chance in the hotel lobby. He'd sought me out.

Leading me into a meeting room, he picks me up and sets me on the edge of a table. "What are you doing here?"

"How did you know I was here?" I hate the idea of lying to him, so I counter with a question of my own.

"We were overseeing the implementation of a new security system." He smiles tightly. I don't need him to explain why it's necessary. Jameson has been gradually increasing security around his hotel, his family, and to my annoyance, his girlfriend, since his dad was killed. "Were you hoping to see me?"

He steps between my legs, angling his face to nuzzle my neck. I hook my arms around his neck, my fingers lingering in his mess of auburn hair. "I'm always hoping to see you, but I had lunch with Monroe."

I'm leaving a few important details out, but I'm not certain he's going to be thrilled about this party. I need to butter him up first.

"Monroe?" he repeats.

"She wants me to feel like part of the family." I prop my index finger over his lips when he tries to speak. "Don't worry. I'm keeping her close without letting her get too close."

"Smart girl," he breathes. Jameson is content with my answer or he's lost his patience. Either way, he's distracted from his interrogation. His hands creep under my shirt to massage my breasts while he kisses my collarbone. Within a few seconds, I'm practically vibrating under his touch.

"You were saying something about friction, Duchess?" he whispers against my skin before brushing his cheek across my neck. My body answers for me, erupting in goosebumps. Jameson chuckles under his breath. He rocks against me and I clutch his tie, lowering my back to the table. I don't bother to ask if he's locked the door, even after he's stripped me from the waist down. One of the perks of being with the owner of a resort is that no one is calling security if they stumble in. Plus, the idea of getting caught sends a throb traveling between my legs.

Jameson's jaw trails along the soft inner skin of my thigh, sending a ripple of pleasure that bubbles out of me in giggles.

"Are you ticklish?" He lingers in the spot until I'm laughing and panting, torn between giddiness and anticipation. Finally, his head pops into view, a smug grin plastered on his face. "You sound like a squeak toy."

I glare at him, too weak from his physical teasing to come up with a retort. My lack of response only encourages him to laugh, too. Hooking his arms around my legs, he drags me to the edge of the table. "Don't worry, Duchess. I'm not done playing with my toy yet."

. . .

Arranging my last visit of the day takes a little more finesse. Explaining to Maddox that I want to visit Monroe's now ex-boyfriend results in a blank stare.

"He got into a fight," I tell him. "He was beaten up pretty badly, and I wanted to check in on him."

"That's considerate of you." Either Maddox isn't buying what I'm selling or he's really more teddy bear than human. I'm happy regardless. As it turns out Maddox is the easy one to appease. Jonas's mother is far less happy to see me.

I smile broadly when she opens the door. "I came to check on Jonas."

"He told me company was coming." It's clear from the way her lips purse like she accidentally sucked on a lemon wedge that he forgot to mention I was the company.

I take her acknowledgment as an invitation and waltz into the house. Unless they've changed things around, I know exactly where his bedroom is. If what Jonas told us was true, then his mom will be thrilled to see a girl going inside.

Well, maybe if that girl was someone other than me. But given my current notoriety, I can't blame her.

Jonas is strung across his bed, absorbed in a PlayStation game.

"I didn't know they still made those," I say. It had been years since I'd played a video game, but, at the moment, I understood the appeal of delaying adolescence.

Jonas looks up and grins. He won't be smiling for much longer, not when I tell him why I'm here. I clutch my purse a little closer. It feels heavier with the police file inside.

"How are you feeling?" I ask, checking out the deep, purple bruises on his cheek bones. A few have begun to fade to green along the edges.

"Fine," he promises. "I think Hugo actually gave me some street cred. My Dad says I look like a real man." Jonas's smile slips and he forces it back on his face, but it no longer reaches his eyes. We both knew that if his father knew the truth, he wouldn't be so proud.

"One more year," I remind him, "and then we can get out of here."

"Not sticking around?" Of course, Jonas remembers my plan to stay in town and run my dad's shop. Because regardless of the mistakes he's made, he's a genuinely decent guy. I'm counting on that decency to help me out.

"I think I'd prefer to get the hell out of town," I say with a laugh.

"I'm glad you aren't staying here," he says conspiratorially, his chocolate brown eyes rich with concern. "This place will poison you—turn you into someone you aren't."

Like someone willing to use anyone and everyone she knows to get what she wants? I try to push my self-disgust down but it keeps rising to the top. If I don't find out who killed Nathaniel West, I'll have the crime hanging over my head for the rest of my life. I tell myself it's not self-service that compels me to use every resource I have to uncover the truth, but rather self-preservation.

"I need your help." I can't stomach sitting here and pretending to be a considerate friend regardless.

Jonas sighs and settles back against his bed. He points to his desk chair, and I take a seat. "I was worried you were going to say that."

"Am I that transparent?" I ask.

"Consider it a good thing. But after all these years, and what I did to you, I don't deserve a house call. That's what gave you away." He winks at me but I see the sorrow hiding in his eyes.

"Maybe you aren't as bad as you think." I pull the folder out of my bag and hold it up. "But you're right I came here for a reason."

"What is that?" he asks, not bothering to get up. In this town, I wouldn't take a nondescript folder either.

"The case file on Nathaniel West's murder." If this is going to work, I have to be completely honest with him. It's a leap of faith to spill my plans to another soul, but I was recently told I needed to be a bit more trusting. I believed Jonas when he said he had nothing to do with the murder, but that's not the reason I've come to him.

"And why do you have it?"

"I paid for it." I toss it on the bed. "You might want to skip the pictures. They're hard to get out of your head."

Jonas doesn't pick it up. "Why are you telling me this, Emma?"

"Because we both know that whoever did this is following your account."

"I'm not posting anymore," he says flatly.

"Look, you created The Dealer to restore some karmic balance to Belle Mère."

"All it did was hurt people," he stops me.

"Then this is your chance to make things right."

"How?" he asks.

"By catching the person who killed Nathaniel West once and for all." I shove a few papers that have fallen out back into the folder. "I'm having a party at the Wests. All I need you to do is post a photo of this in the office."

"Where he was killed?" Jonas's face is ashen.

"Whoever did it will know it's a message. They'll come looking for the file."

"And you'll catch them red-handed." Jonas pauses to considerate, then he shakes his head. "You can't be sure they're still following the account."

"They are," I say firmly.

"But how do you know?" He doesn't share my certainty, but that's not important.

"I know they'll come looking for one reason, because they haven't been caught yet."

"You aren't as clever as you think you are," Maddox says, drawing my attention away from my cell phone after we leave Jonas's house.

"What?"

"Running around town, whipping everyone into a frenzy. I know you're up to something." He keeps his eyes on the road, occasionally checking his blind spots. Maddox is always watching. Of course, he saw through my errands.

I have a choice: keep trying to lie to him or get him on

my side. Considering I'm not the one paying his salary, he has no real reason to keep quiet—unless I give him one.

"Fine," I level with him. "I am up to something, but it's the only way to clear all our names."

"And what happens when you catch who did it? What if it's one of you?" he asks bluntly.

That's the second time today I've been forced to face that possibility, but it doesn't lessen my resolve. "It wasn't me and it wasn't Jameson."

He chuckles. "So everyone else is on their own?"

The photos of the crime scene flash through my mind. Jameson found his father like that. No matter what had passed between them, he had faced that gruesome discovery. Someone left his father for him to find, and that person is going to pay.

Pawnography's newest sales associate waves to me from behind the counter. There's something comforting about knowing that she's here to keep the store in check. The shop is swarming with customers, which is its new normal following the media storm that is my life Suddenly, my impulse to retrieve the Venetian mask I bought ages ago feels foolish. Tugging the tie from my ponytail I let my hair fall like a curtain over my face. If this keeps up, I'm going to have to invest in a wardrobe of over-sized sunglasses and wide-brimmed hats. I ninja through the crowd, careful not to make eye contact with any of the patrons. Most of their attention is on the items under the glass and the girl behind the counter.

I blend in, so no one notices me, but I stop in my tracks when a woman bustles up to Josie at the counter. She's dressed in a Las Vegas t-shirt that screams tourist. Judging from her mom jeans, she's a Midwesterner. In my experience Kansans love a good souvenir shirt and a pair of high-waters. I suspect that if she turns around, there will be a fanny pack buckled around her ample waistline.

"Where's the girl?" she demands.

Josie blinks innocently, but I can tell by how forcefully she stares the woman down that she knows exactly what she's asking. "I'm sorry?"

"The girl they keep talking about on television and the world-wide web." The customer twirls her hand impatiently as if a nondescript gesticulation will help clarify her point.

"She doesn't work here." Josie smiles as she delivers the bad news, and I want to hug her.

"The television said she works her." The woman pulls out her phone and I groan inwardly. "Look at this article. That's this shop."

"Yes, it is," Josie confirms.

"So, where is she?"

"I'm sorry, but if you would like to make a purchase—"

"I came all the way from Nebraska..."

Nebraska. Kansas. What's the difference? I lose interest as the woman continues her tirade. After a few minutes a weary looking man retrieves her with an apologetic look to Josie.

"The internet said she works here," the woman reminds him angrily.

"I know."

"She needs to repent for her sins. I came here..."

I'm saved from hearing exactly why she came here as the couple exit the shop without their prize.

"Didn't want to give them an autograph?" Josie whispers conspiratorially. She tugs at the hem of her green tank top self-consciously and I do my best not to look. "That was conspicuous."

"What?" I hold up my hands.

"The baby bump check you just did. I'm not showing. Mom just shrunk this shirt," Josie explains.

"I wasn't looking." But I guess I can't lie to her.

"I have an appointment." Josie keeps her voice low so that no one can overhear. "It can't get here fast enough."

On the outside with her stylish, dark curls, and fuchsia lipstick, Josie plays the part of a grown woman, but I can see the fear she'd trying to hide. I can't blame her. If it were me in her shoes, I'd be freaking out. I hesitate, uncertain how she'll feel about my next question. "Can I go with you?"

"If you want." She shrugs but I don't miss how her lower lip trembles. That's a definite yes.

"So, are you coming to my party?" I decide a change of topic is in order. I haven't had the chance to give her the lowdown on my plan to catch Nathaniel West's murderer at my birthday bash, so I distract her with the info now.

"Yes, but explain to me why we're having a party there? Isn't that the last place you would want to celebrate your birthday?"

"Can't a girl throw a rager for her eighteenth birthday? I can legally vote. It's time to celebrate." I slide along the glass case, looking for what I came in for. When I spot the mask, I tap the spot. "I'm going to need that."

Josie takes it from the case and raises an eyebrow. "What are you up to?"

It's a fair point, but not one I can explain without a lot more time and possibly some visual aids. "If you promise to come, I promise you'll find out."

"You're being very mysterious." She wraps it in some paper and hands me the bag.

"Aren't I?" I tease. "Oh, you're going to need one of these, too."

"Like a costume?"

Before I can tell her anymore, a customer butts in. I'm relieved when he asks to see an autographed baseball card in the case instead of wanting to take a photo with me. The longer I stick around the shop, the more chance there is that I'll be recognized.

"I'll text you," I promise, waving goodbye.

Pushing open the glass security door, I escape from that life and return to the one I've chosen. To outsiders my decision to host a masquerade ball in honor of my eighteenth birthday signals that I've just becoming another showy Houser. I think it's one of my more brilliant ideas, though. What better safety net could you offer a murderer if you were hoping they'd come to call?

By the weekend, Monroe has acquired every bottle of good champagne in Las Vegas. I stare at the lines of bottles displayed on the bar. The previous shindig I'd crashed had utilized the West's private stock of liquor.

"Why do we need this much champagne again?" I ask.

"For the theme," she says as if this makes perfect sense. "I'm going for nouveau riche. Think *The Great Gatsby* meets trailer park." She sweeps her hand in the air as if to share her vision.

"Have I told you you're a bitch today?" I ask, crossing my arms.

"Not today." She bats her eyelashes like I've paid her a compliment. Knowing Monroe, I have.

"You're a bitch."

She ignores me and begins to point out various details I couldn't care less about. I nod when appropriate, but she isn't buying it. "This party was your idea."

I shrug. I could care less if she's taken it over. I had expected her to when I pitched the idea. I need Monroe to play hostess because she was the one who invited the guests earlier this summer. All of that is important to me. I just don't give a damn about the drinks or the decorations.

"Your outfit is in Jameson's room," she says, clearly washing her hands of me. "Go get dressed."

"I'm wearing this." I gesture to the flowing, yellow maxi I put on this morning. It's simple but comfortable, and tonight I'll have enough attention directed at me no matter what I wear.

"Don't argue with me," she snaps. "If you're going to be a West, you need to dress like one."

"But won't I look more nouveau riche in this?" I ask flatly.

"I'm making Jameson wear a tuxedo, you'll be underdressed," she informs me. The change in tactics works. It's hard enough to hold a candle next to him. If the right clothes can help ease the feeling of inferiority I'm apt to fall victim to I should take her up on the offer.

"How did your mom feel about the party?" I ask Monroe as she signs a delivery sheet.

"She's not thrilled," Monroe admits, "but she'll get over it."

"I want her to like me." Immediately, I wish I hadn't shared that snippet with Monroe. In her world, information is power.

"She does," Monroe says to my surprise. "I told her the party was my idea."

"Why would you do that?" I've watched how critical Evelyn West can be of her daughter's choices this summer. Letting her mom believe it's her idea to host a party in the same space where her dad was murdered didn't seem like the best plan.

"Strategy. Mom wants us to get along, so I told her I was dying to throw you a birthday party."

"In other words, you lied?" I ask.

"Yes. My mother is a sucker for lies if it paints the picture she wants to see. She's too eager to watch us bond to cause trouble."

"So she actually likes me?" Despite the kindness Jameson's mother has shown me, I had to wonder if her opinion of me had reversed in light of our "engagement."

"Yes, Pollyanna," Monroe confirms dryly. "She thinks you hung the moon."

Armed with this good news, I surrender to Monroe's request and dismiss myself to dress, which has the added benefit of getting me away from the party planning. The outfit, or lack of it, that she's picked out for me is laid out on Jameson's bed.

Band-aids have more surface area than this thing, and don't get me started on the lacy scraps of string that accompany it. The tiny dress is covered in gold sequins that sparkle luminously in the light. When I lift it from the bed, I discover a gorgeous mask hiding underneath. I had planned on wearing the one I picked up at Pawnography, but I can't help but admire the one Monroe has selected. The mask itself is made of a creamy porcelain with subtle facial features painted on in gold. The gilt effect around the eyes looks like long feathers. I hold it up to my face and peer through the openings.

The heat of my breath collects inside it, but there's something comforting about having the mask on. Behind this, I can be Emma Southerly again instead of Jameson's girlfriend or murder suspect or gold digger. With this on, none of those labels seem to stick. There's liberation in deception.

I place the mask gently onto the nightstand and begin to strip. I'll have to do something with my hair, but makeup won't be as important if I stay hidden all night. I hadn't considered that perk of a masquerade party. Squirming into the dress, I realize that it's not compatible with my current underwear. My gaze strays to the thong I've left on the bed.

"Seriously?" I say to myself.

A soft laugh startles me and I pivot to find Jameson standing the doorway.

"Do you knock?" I ask, trying to tug up the stuck zipper.

"It's my room," he reminds me. He pushes the door closed behind him.

"I'll knock next time." I give up on the zipper and cross my arms over my chest.

"You're in a mood," he notes as he comes closer. When he reaches me, he runs the back of his hand down my arm. The effect of his touch is both soothing and exciting.

"This party is a terrible idea," I admit. "Is it too late to cancel?"

"And disappoint all those people who want to be your friends now?"

Jameson has no idea the real reason that I've planned this gathering tonight. The more people who know, the worse are chances are of catching the murderer. But as the party gets closer, I'm beginning to wonder if it's a good idea at all. What if I'm wrong? I'll be exposing myself and Jonas to even more scrutiny from the police.

A pit opens in my stomach as I consider an even worse possibility: what if I don't want to know who killed Nathaniel West?

"None of the people coming tonight matter," he continues, mistaking my silence as hesitance. "If you want to cancel, then we will. Although might I request you wear this dress tonight regardless."

"I don't think I can wear this dress period," I say absently, picking up the collection of strings I'm pretty certain are supposed to be underwear. "I mean, look at this! Why bother?"

Jameson adjusts his collar with one hand. "You should give them a fair chance."

"Oh yeah?"

He takes them from me and dangles them off his index finger. "You should definitely give these a chance."

"Aren't you worried about me bending over?" I ask.

"I'll just have to stay behind you all night and keep the view to myself."

It's too late to call tonight off, and I can't freak myself out a second longer, so when Jameson backs me toward his bedroom wall, I don't resist. His breath is hot on my neck as he trails his lips down to the curve of my shoulder.

"When is this party?" he whispers.

"Who cares?" I breathe.

Jameson's hands bunch my flimsy skirt around my waist as he presses his body against mine. "That's the right answer, Duchess."

WHEN JOSIE ARRIVES AN HOUR LATER, I'm in a much better mood. The party doesn't start for another hour but she's already dressed in a slinky, red wrap dress. The mask she's chosen is the same brilliant crimson.

"Va va voom!" I exclaim when she parks herself in the kitchen. Monroe's made it clear that I'm not to touch anything. I've been cut out of the party planning entirely. Instead, I'm stealing nibbles from the food trays.

Josie holds up her mask so I can see the two tiny horns protruding from the top. "I'm going for she-devil."

"And winning," I assure her, offering her a tiny sandwich from a fancy, silver platter.

She takes one and pops the whole thing in her mouth. Then she gives a thumbs up. "You didn't tell me this party was going to be so..."

"Over-the-top?" I suggest.

"Actually I was thinking serious. Passed hors d'oeuvres and champagne. It's a little different from..." she trails away as horror slackens her face.

"We thought we'd try something a little different." I shrug my shoulders to show she hasn't wrecked the evening by mentioning that the only other party she had been to here was on the night of the murder. I, on the other hand, had crashed another a few weeks later, but only by accident. Those parties had been the equivalent of a rich kid's kegger not the dressed-up event we'd concocted this evening. Maybe the subterfuge aspect had appealed to Monroe on some personal wavelength. Either way she'd gone out of her way to make this a memorable evening, and if I had my way, it would be even more so. "Or Monroe did at least."

At the mention of her name the blonde flies through the kitchen like a demonic fireball. "Have you seen the menu cards?"

Josie and I help her search until we've tracked them

down. She hardly notices that Josie is here, even after my best friend discovers where the cards have been put.

"She's crankier than usual." Josie purses her lips thoughtfully, and I can't help but realize that she has a point. Monroe is acting strangely.

"In all fairness, I used blackmail to get her to throw this party," I admit.

Josie links her arm through mine. "Do tell."

It isn't my secret, but the gossip is too good not to share. I've kept Monroe's hidden life quiet from her family and friends. But Josie isn't her family or her friend. She's mine, and I trust her.

"Promise not to tell," I ask.

"Cross my heart and hope to die." Josie slashes her fingers over her chest for emphasis.

I dish the dirt in whispers. Josie's eyes widen until I think they're going to bulge out. When I finish, she shakes her head. "You must have been pretty scary?"

"Why would you say that?" I'm a bit offended by the idea.

"Because she's acting like her whole life is riding on this. She must be worried that you're going to rat her out."

There's no reason Monroe should believe that. I'd used the information I'd had as leverage, but if I'd wanted to tattle, I would have done so. I make up my mind to keep a closer eye on my adoptive sister this evening. After all, she's not the only one with a lot riding on tonight.

No one is late to the party. When the doors ceremonially open at 8:30, every student at Belle Mere Prep is waiting. Security does a decent job weeding undercover reporters from the crowd, but my heartbeat speeds up as I survey the group of strangers before me. Behind their masks, I can't recognize any of them, and I realize without their masks, I wouldn't know most of them anyway. The uppermost floor of West Casino has been transformed into a golden playground. Ropes of sparking lights drip from the ceiling, casting a warm glow that feels out of place in the modern setting. Dozens of white roses dipped in gold-leaf are staged strategically throughout the space.

"It's gorgeous," Josie says as she comes up beside.

"It's gaudy," I correct her. "Actually, it's nouveau riche."

The whole scene screams wealth and debauchery.

Monroe has made her point. In the future, if I'm going to fit in I might try to do so with a bit less theatricality.

"What?" Josie asks.

"Inside joke," I say dryly. I haven't had the heart to tell Josie how much money Hans put in my trust fund before he went upriver. Between my relationship with Jameson and everything going on in her private life, I don't want the gulf between us to widen any further.

"When did that happen?" she shrieks. I follow her finger to find Hugo and Leighton entering, hand in hand.

Leave it to him to be the only person late to the party of the century. Behind my mask I study the way Hugo hovers near Leighton. I can't imagine what it took to convince him to let her come back here. Not after she'd nearly died. Glancing over I realize I can't even tell which window we went through. It's been repaired—erased as if it never happened.

"I didn't tell you? They were together when I went to the hospital. He's been there since she woke up."

"I did not call that," Josie admits, waving her hand under her mask. "Screw this."

She pulls off her mask and smiles tightly.

"Too hot?" I ask.

"Yeah. Besides no one here knows who I am anyway. My face is as good as a mask," she says with a laugh.

I don't miss the pain that lingers in her eyes. Josie has never felt like she belongs here. I can't imagine how she feels at the moment.

"Let's find you some water," I suggest, but before I can

abscond with her to the kitchen, a man steps into our path. "Excuse me."

He catches me around the waist when I try to push past him. Tipping his masked face lower, he whispers, "You don't recognize me, Duchess?"

"Of course, I do." My fingers trace the broad shoulders accentuated by the dark cashmere of his tuxedo jacket. "You're supposed to be watching my back."

Literally and figuratively.

"A West is always fashionably late," he advises me, pushing his mask up. He points to the corridor that leads to the private family rooms. "Case in point."

Monroe is the last to arrive, despite the obsessive care she took planning it. She sweeps into the room in a long black gown that dips low, exposing the valley between her breasts. Unlike the mask she chose for me, hers is a simple lace strip tied around her eyes. Monroe West is on display for all of us to see, but how many people see past the image she projects?

Josie clears her throat to remind us that she's still here. "I'll give you two some space."

Before I can tear myself away from Jameson to join her, Monroe marches up to us.

"How did they get past security?" she hisses, pointing to Sabine, her former best friend, and Levi, Jameson's former roommate. She's not the only one late to the party.

"Were they on the list?" Jameson asks indifferently. He's much more calm than the last time he was in the same room as Levi. He's had time to cope with his fair-weather friend's betrayal.

"How can you just stand there?" Monroe demands, and I can't help but agree with her.

"That movie will never get made. Levi will continue to be a B-list star whose destiny depends on his looks. Karma has done its part as far as I'm concerned."

"You're a bigger person than I am." Monroe sweeps across the room after them.

I tug Jameson's arm, forcing him to follow.

"My sister can fight her own battles," he reassures me, but I ignore him.

"You broke it, you bought it."

I have no idea how Sabine and Levi got up here," he says gruffly. "Security has been notified that they can't so much as step foot on the sidewalk."

"And yet, they're here." Judging from Monroe's reaction, they wouldn't be for much longer. A chilling thought occurs to me as we approach them. If it was that easy for two people to crash this party after all the security upgrades that had been made since Nathaniel's death, how many other people can get past the surveillance and guards —tonight and the night of the murder?

As we approach the threesome, we're joined by Hugo and Leighton. My pulse speeds up and I clutch Jameson's hand. I'd once considered them the Belle Mere axis of evil. Circumstances had torn them apart this summer, which means there's no way to know how ugly this argument could get.

"You weren't invited." Monroe delivers her dismissal in a lowered voice, but Sabine only laughs at her.

"I know every staff member of this hotel. I'm always invited." Sabine has eschewed the traditional uniform of pink I usually see her in. Instead, she's rocking an electric blue number and a silver, Venetian carnival mask. Next to her Levi shifts on his heels.

Jameson doesn't bother to tell his former friend that he's unwelcome. He handed down that edict when he first learned that Levi planned to play him in a damning biopic. The role would have made Levi's career. Now the movie was dead in the water along with their friendship.

The tilt of Jameson's head is hardly perceptible but a few moments later, Maddox appears behind our small group.

"Mr. Stone, please follow me."

Levi shoots Jameson a pleading look, but it's too little too late. Sabine stays frozen in place even as her boyfriend follows our hulking private muscle toward the elevator.

"Monroe," Sabine begins, but Monroe holds up her palm.

"Leave," she commands.

"What's going on with you two?" Leighton interjects. She doesn't bother to keep her voice quiet, and all around us, heads turn. Apparently, she's still a little hazy on what's happened in her absence. I glare at Hugo accusatorily. He brought her here knowing full well that their little friendship circle is broken forever.

"Tell her," Sabine says, stamping her heel on the tile.

Now the whole party is watching. "Tell her what's going on with us, Monroe."

"It's best you go." Monroe turns but not before Sabine moves closer.

"Tell her who pushed her out the window."

A low buzz breaks out around us as people figure out what she's saying.

"Get her out of here," Monroe shouts to the security guards who are standing by hesitantly.

"No." Hugo steps in. "I want to hear what she has to say."

"Tell them," Sabine sneers. She might lose the war but she's going to win this battle and it seems there will be casualties.

"It was a misunderstanding," Monroe begins, her eyes flash to each of us. No doubt she's hoping one of us will save her. The trouble is that none of us have reason to.

"You pushed her through the window," Hugo screams, and I'm reminded of how swiftly he'd turned on someone he considers his best friend. It doesn't matter if Monroe did it so long as Hugo believes she did.

Before I can nudge Jameson to intervene, Jonas steps out from the crowd. More than anyone, he doesn't owe Monroe any favors. But when Hugo takes a purposeful step toward her, Jonas grabs him from behind.

"Let's cool off," he coaxes his best friend.

"Why? Because I can't hit a girl?" Hugo asks. "Because she's no lady. She's a cold-blooded bitch. You know that."

"Drop it," Jonas urges, struggling to keep his hold as

Hugo thrashes. After a few moments, Hugo goes limp. But before we can breathe a collective sigh of relief. He casts a scornful glare at Monroe. "Assault. Prostitution. What else are you capable of, Madam West?"

The accusation goes off like a bomb and the low murmurs of gossip die down as everyone strains to hear her response. Looking around, I realize more than a few people have been filming this encounter. Within hours, Monroe West's private life will be subject to an online smear campaign.

Monroe raises her chin in defiance and then she does the last thing any of us expects: she shrugs.

"Caught me," she says with a wicked smirk. Next to me Jameson doesn't move. I'd wondered before if he knew what she was up to, and now I know. He had no clue.

Security finally does their job and escorts Sabine to the elevator. Hugo begins to follow but Leighton just stands there staring. Monroe doesn't meet her minion's eyes until Leighton's soft voice calls for her attention.

"It was you. Emma told me I saw someone that night and that I smiled at them before we went through the window." She repeats the story I told her as if she's finally remembering. "You tried to kill me."

"I overreacted," Monroe admits, and more than a few people around us boo her. When this news leaks, she'll be the talk of the town. The question is whether or not her temper flared up so dramatically on the night her father was murdered. I can't be the only one wondering that now.

But despite the demonstration of what she's capable of,

somehow I know it wasn't her. Monroe and Jameson didn't hate their father regardless of his faults. Rational or not, Monroe had a reason for why she'd pushed us out the window that night. What would make her hurt her father? All these people surrounding us now were there as well. The room is full of opportunity, but I still can't find the motive?

Monroe seems to realize that she's playing to a crowd that's turned on her, so she beats a hasty retreat.

"I need to talk to my sister," Jameson says, his voice so frigid that a chill runs down my spine. He follows her away from the crowd and I contemplate stepping in. Monroe certainly owes me an apology, although I don't want her explanations. The reasons behind her actions are quite clear to me. In the end, I stay put, watching as most of my top suspects take the elevator. They'd all been hiding something, but if they aren't the ones behind the murder, who is?

As the crowd begins to disperse, waiting for whatever unexpected entertainment comes next, Jonas steps beside me.

"We have a problem."

It's the last thing I want to hear. He gestures for me to follow him. As soon as we're in an empty corridor, he levels with me.

"It's gone," he says.

"What's gone?" I ask even as dread floods through me. I don't wait for him to say it before I rushing down the hall to Nathaniel West's office.

The FBI had unsealed the room weeks ago, but I hadn't bothered to come in here. Not even when I arrived to prepare for the party this morning. That had been Jonas's job. I considered it remuneration for the emotional distress he caused me when he posted photos of me online.

The office is as Spartan as ever, but I ransack the drawers anyway. "Maybe a maid came along and put it away."

"Emma, it's not there," he insists. "I checked."

"Then where could it possibly be?" Stress seizes my chest, making me feel as though I'm in a choke hold. Without that file, we have nothing.

"As soon as I got here, I checked to make sure you'd left it where you were supposed to," he explains. "But when I came back a few minutes ago, it was gone."

"Did you get the picture? Did you post it?"

He shakes his head and my heart sinks, drowning my hopes along with it. "Without the bait..."

"Emma," Jonas says slowly, his brown eyes nearly black in the dark, "could someone have known it was here?"

"No. I didn't tell anyone else." Panic gets the better of me and I kick the desk chair. Most of my suspects just walked out of the casino lobby, and, like it or not, none of them seemed capable of murder. They were all too caught up in their problems. "We're missing something."

I think for a moment before I hold out my hand. "Let me see your phone."

Jonas unlocks the screen and hands it to me. He

already has The Dealer account pulled up. So much for the best laid plans. I scroll through, studying each picture.

"Why these people?" I ask him. There'd been dozens of party-goers there the night that Nathaniel was murdered, but Jonas had only focused his attention on a handful.

"Hunches. Weird behavior. Bias," he admits.

As I look at the stream, I notice something that hadn't occurred to me before. Naturally, I'd gravitated toward analyzing photos of myself and Jameson. People I didn't trust were already suspects in my book. That left one person whose presence in the stream I'd hardly questioned.

"You said you wanted to deal out some karma." It was a desire I understood. I'd been the victim of Monroe and her posse's bullying, and I'd fallen prey to Hugo Roth's playboy antics. That didn't explain everyone who'd caught The Dealer's attention. "What did Josie do to deserve such a prominent feature on your thread?"

"It's not only about karma," he says slowly. "I guess I wanted to expose what people try to keep hidden."

So, he knew Josie's secret, or one of them. He'd posted pictures of her with older men. Since he'd followed her to the family planning clinic, Jonas had probably guessed the other item Josie wanted to keep undercover.

"That wasn't your right," I say through gritted teeth. "Josie has issues..."

I feel like a turncoat for even speaking the words, but it's the truth. I don't understand how Jonas can't see that.

His own parents had rejected who he was. Josie didn't even have a father to reject her.

"I wanted to figure out who killed Nathaniel West, so I couldn't ignore her."

"She was barely at the party." I'm really losing my cool now.

Why? the tiny voice in my head asks, but I ignore it.

"I saw her late that night," he corrects me. "Nearly everyone had gone home or passed out, but she was running. She looked totally wrecked. I tried to go after her but Monroe stopped me. I knew you two hadn't been invited, so I distracted Monroe so there wouldn't be a scene."

I can feel my heart slowing down as his words sink in. "Are you saying that Josie—"

"Knows who killed Nathaniel West?" he finishes my thought. "I'm sure she does."

There's no time to consider any of the questions flooding through me as I run out of the office. But despite telling myself there is rational explanation, I can't help but wonder how I've been so blind. Rushing into the party, I search for Josie's red mask in the crowd. Following Monroe's exit, the drinking has begun in earnest. More than a few champagne bottles lie empty on their sides, and as I stand there I jump when more corks are popped. The hired waiters have given up in the face of mob mentality.

They're celebrating Monroe's overthrow. I don't miss the irony that she provided the champagne they're using to toast her demise. It will take all the West's people to clean up this mess. I can only guess that Jameson is still addressing the debacle privately. But right now I need him at my side.

I've fucked this up royally, and he's the only person I trust to know what to do.

Jonas appears at my side, and I resist the urge to strangle him. Why hadn't he told me about seeing Josie at the party? Why hadn't he told anyone?

Because he'd been scared like she is now. He'd misunderstood that fear. We both had.

Without knowing where Jameson is, he'll do—but only in a pinch.

"I need to find Josie. She's wearing a red dress and a red mask." I leave him to search through the crowd while I go to find Jameson. I'm halfway to the family bedrooms when I hear raised voices. I pause. They're coming from the room across the hall from his.

I don't bother to knock.

Monroe looks up with tear-stained eyes and runny mascara when I enter. She opens her mouth to order me out, but I cut her off.

"I need you now," I tell Jameson.

"Can this wait?" he asks as we step into the hall. "I'm not done crucifying my sister."

"Nail her to the cross in the morning. I need you. I fucked up."

Jameson's face goes blank and he doesn't speak, which is probably a good thing since it's all pouring out now.

"I made a mistake. I thought I could smoke out the murderer, but I was wrong. And now, I can't take it back."

Jameson grabs me by the shoulders and looks me dead in the eye. "What's going on?"

"We were wrong," I continue, the first hysterical sob breaking loose. "It wasn't murder. It couldn't be."

"Emma, you aren't making sense."

I force my mouth closed then I inhale deeply. When I speak again, I keep it simple. "We have to find Josie."

He doesn't ask questions, although I'm certain he has as many as I do. Maybe he's responding to my panic or perhaps he has simply kicked into crisis mode. Grabbing my hand, we join the crush of people partying. He doesn't let go as we weave in and out.

When I see a red mask, I yank it off without looking. But none of the red masks are hers. When we make it to the other side of the crowd, we huddle together.

"Did you see her?" he asks.

I shake my head as my breathing speeds up.

"Calm down," he orders me. "What is going on?"

"I don't have time to explain!"

"Then give me the CliffsNotes," he recommends.

"I might have gotten ahold of the police file for your dad's murder." I don't stop to see how he reacts to this information. "I convinced Jonas to use The Dealer to bait the murderer."

"You did what?"

"It was reckless. I realize that now, but I thought it was the only way." I'm screwing up this whole explanation thing, but I'm too distracted by the possible consequences of what I've done to care.

"What does this have to do with Josie?"

"I think she has the file." I can't bring myself to admit why I think she took it.

Jameson seems to understand though. "We'll find her. She's going to be okay."

How can he say that? How can anything ever be okay again? But I'm reminded of the inscription on the ring I wear. If ever I need to take a leap of faith, it's now. He leads me around the bar and past a security guard stationed to prevent unauthorized guests from entering the private spaces of his home. The guard is busy flirting with a few drunk girls I recognize as a year younger than me.

"Has anyone been through here?" Jameson demands as the guard jumps to his feet.

"Only our people."

"Who?" I press. I no longer know who to count as our people. The distinctions between friends and strangers feels more acute than ever before.

"Steve and your guy, Maddox. But they took off." I can see the gears whirring in his head as he searches his memory. "And your friend."

My blood turns to ice and it takes all the strength I have to respond. "The one in the red dress?"

He nods.

She'd been here before the party. She had been in Jameson's bedroom. We'd snacked in the kitchen. Of course, the guards would see her as an authorized friend of the family.

"Where was she going?"

As soon as he points in the direction of the kitchen, I take off running with Jameson at my heels. A few members of the wait staff stare when we round the corner. She isn't here. Whipping around, I consider where she might have gone.

"If she came for the file, would she leave?" Jameson asks.

"I don't know." Taking it wouldn't destroy the evidence that it contains. After all, it's only a copy. But she'd come. I'd been wrong earlier when I told Jonas that no one else knew about our plan. Josie knew.

Because I had told her.

She knew it was a trap and she'd walked into it. The realization nearly knocks me off my feet. Jameson catches me as I stumble and that's when I spot the black and white photo caught in the track of the sliding door.

Forcing myself forward, I open it and step onto the patio. The night is unusually still. This high up I might expect a breeze, but nothing disturbs the scene I find. Photos and affidavits litter the concrete as if they've been strewn along like breadcrumbs.

She's leading me straight to her. I spot a dot of red in the pool and I run toward the water. I fall before I reach it, scraping my knees on the pavement.

Jameson makes it all the way, but he stops at the edge. "It's just a mask."

I cry out with relief and then force myself to stand. I have to find her. When my gaze falls on her, I freeze. She's perched on the rail of the balcony with her back to us as she looks out over the strip below.

"Josie," I call out tentatively.

She glances over her shoulder and gives me a sad smile. It's all the encouragement I need to step closer.

"You came," she says. "I knew you would."

"Whatever happened, everything is going to be okay."

Her laughter comes out as a harsh bark. "Tell me, Jameson"—she moves, twisting on the slippery metal railing and my heart stops until she's turned herself around to face us—"is it okay? I killed your father. Is that okay?"

I can't bring myself to look at him, so I stand there between the two people I love most in the world while the truth slowly tears us apart.

"I think I understand. He was your father, too, wasn't he?" Jameson's voice is steady and sympathetic, and for the first time since the horrible realization dawned on me, I believe it can be okay.

"You need to know...I didn't know that," she says as a tear streaks down her cheek. "I didn't plan this."

"We know that," I tell her. "Let's talk about this." I beckon for her to come down, but her hands tighten on the railing.

"No one knows the truth but us. It can stay that way," Jameson promises her.

"You really are the brother I never had." She sniffles, hesitating for a moment as if to consider his offer. "But you don't know the truth."

"I do," I say. I've pieced it together in fragments.

"I was looking for you." She turns her attention to me. "We got separated and...I didn't mean to wind up in his office. But when I did he was nothing like I expected. He wanted me there. I knew why. I've had enough older men try to take me home."

I nod encouragingly. She needs to confess so that we can all move on.

"You know I never slept with any of those guys," she admits. "I'd let them buy me dinner and feel me up."

I take a step closer. If I reach out I can grab her. "You were a virgin."

It's not a question. It's a fact.

"I'm all talk. After all these years, even people don't know the rumors about me." She tilts her head up as if looking into heaven. "I was tired of being all talk. And I was tired of being treated like dirt. We weren't invited to that party. Did she tell you that?"

"Yes," Jameson says. He hasn't moved. No doubt he doesn't want to frighten her. He, far more than me, holds the absolution she needs to receive.

"We both met the men that would change our lives." An unexpected gust of wind whips her skirt around her legs, and I leap forward afraid it will push her over. She holds up a hand to stop me.

"Josie, please come down," I beg her.

She ignores me. "I didn't put up a fight. I wanted it. I wanted to look Monroe West in the eyes and know I screwed her daddy. I told myself that she didn't deserve any of it, and that all I wanted was a taste."

"He was rough." Her eyes grow distant, rewinding back to that fateful night. "But I didn't cry. He told me he liked that—that I was a good girl."

"Why?" Jameson finally chokes out. "What did he do to you?"

"He asked for my name. He wanted to call me, and I just didn't care anymore. I thought maybe I'd get taken care of for once, so I told him my name. Josie Deckard. I'll never forget the look on his face when he asked me if Marion Deckard was my mother. When I said yes, he lost it. He grabbed me and he asked me why I was there. He wanted to know if I'd come on purpose. How I'd found out. I don't think he knew he was hurting me," she says softly. "I don't think I realized I'd grabbed the letter opener. When he accused me of coming there to fuck him for more of his money, I didn't understand. Not until he asked me what kind of sick girl screws her father."

I clamp my hand over my mouth to hold back the sobs threatening to escape. Now I understood her erratic behavior over the last few months. Josie had wanted to meet her father her whole life. No one could have expected the truth.

"I can't remember much, except for the way his skin popped when the blade struck him. I hear it all the time. I still feel the way it vibrated across my skin each time I stabbed him. And then I ran and waited for them to come for me."

"No one's coming for you," I say, hoping it will reassure her.

"They should. I've stood by and watched while they accused you. I've been too scared to make a move. Even when I found out I was pregnant, and I couldn't lie to myself about what happened, I was stuck."

Her admission startles Jameson, who lurches back a few steps. I'd kept her pregnancy from him because it wasn't his business. Now he's facing it at the worst possible moment.

"What do you think of me now?" she asks him. "Am I so easy to forgive?"

I hold my breath as I wait for his answer.

"Yes," he says. "I forgive you."

"We're going to make it through this." I hold out my hand and she lifts her slowly, her eyes brimming with tears. "We'll take care of things."

"No, you won't." She shakes her head, her hand still hovering within reach. "My mom used to tell me that we make our own beds. Mine's a mess, Em."

"All of ours are," I reassure her.

"I've got to clean it up. You understand, don't you?"

I nod, inching toward her. "I'll help you."

She laughs and the emptiness of it fills the quiet night. "Deckard girls don't ask for help, remember?"

"Josie!"

She smiles one last time, and then she lets go.

A thick blanket wraps around my shoulders. I blink as Jameson swims into focus, the night sky a black canvas overhead. No stars twinkle above as if they've gone silent, too.

"You're trembling," Jameson explains.

"I am?" I hadn't noticed.

He rubs my shoulders, allowing me to sit quietly in the midst of chaos. I'm aware of the officers and agents sweeping the scene for evidence. I wince as a camera flashes, but I don't move.

I'd collapsed there moments after it happened and I still can't bring myself to get up. Not while strangers piece together the last few moments of my best friend's life.

A medic comes over and explains that I might be in shock. I nod, not bothering to tell him that I don't care. When he suggests that I lie on a stretcher, Jameson intervenes.

"She's fine," he says firmly.

"It would be best if—"

Jameson cuts the man off before he can get any farther. "I know what's best for her."

I stare at him and then slowly I lift my hand to his. I need him to anchor me while my world spins out of control. Later, we'll discuss what happened. Later, we'll deal with it.

Later, I'll feel something other than numbness.

The silence is interrupted by the click of heels across concrete. I can hear each purposeful step coming closer. Jameson straightens, but I don't bother to look up.

"Emma." Agent Mackey's voice is unusually gentle. I find myself wishing she would scream. "We have a few questions."

"I'll be happy to talk with you later," Jameson interrupts.

"We really need statements from both of you." She's straining to keep her voice soft. She wants to scream.

I don't blame her.

"We can arrange for her to make a statement in a few days."

"Given the situation, I would think you'd be eager to get this behind you," Mackey finally snaps, unleashing her inner dragon.

"It is behind us," Jameson says, his tone remaining even, "which is why my lawyers will be in touch in a few days."

"Mr. West," she starts.

"You can speak with my lawyers." He leans down so that only I can hear. "I want to take you home."

"I don't have a home," I mumble. At most, I've always had pillars, and now that one of them has fallen, I can't stand on my own.

"I'm your home," he reminds me. "Do you want me to carry you?"

When I don't answer, he lifts me into his arms and carries me away from this nightmare. He drives us into the mountains to the closest thing either of us has to a home.

That night he holds me against him. No words pass between us, even though neither of us sleep. The clock on the nightstand slowly counts the minutes and I watch each one drain away. One moment snuffed out for eternity. When the first light of dawn slashes across the horizon, it seems impossible that the sun will ever rise again.

It does anyway.

Dr. O'Donnell never asks me how I feel, which is the only reason I continue to see her.

Her office is decorated with framed Rorschach tests. I still can't decide if the one hanging over her desk is a dog or an elephant. She won't tell me what that means.

She takes her seat across from the couch and crosses her legs. There's no notepad and I don't lie down. Mostly, we talk.

"Have you cried?" she asks gently.

I shake my head. I'd cried at the funeral. Seeing Marion bury her daughter had broken me into pieces so small that there's no room for tears any longer.

"How are you feeling about tomorrow?"

"I'm not really," I admit. Part of the reason I agreed to go to therapy the numbness that hadn't abated since the night Josie jumped.

"Part of what you're coping with is a sense of futility," she explains. "Everything feels inevitable."

"Isn't it?" I ask. Life. Death. Taxes. I couldn't escape any of it.

"Have you spoken to your mom?"

"She's coming to grips with my pseudo-engagement." After everything went down, Mom went through a sudden bout of maternal paranoia. She refused to accept the seriousness of my relationship with Jameson, but she stopped demanding I move in with her. "And she's finally packed up all of Hans's things."

Mentioning my stepfather doesn't move me either. I'm just as numb to what he did.

"How is Jameson?" she broaches the one topic that never fails to elicit an emotional reaction.

I smile begrudgingly. "Perfect."

She knew this, of course. He'd been seeing her for the past few weeks as well. While my therapy consisted of open-ended questions and encouragement, he'd chosen a more proactive path.

"I have to ask, Emma, are you certain you want to return to Belle Mère tomorrow?"

O'Donnell isn't the type to worry, but there's concern in her voice. Given that I'm a walking time bomb, I can't blame her.

"Yes." I have other options, but I don't want to cut and run. "It's not the first time I'll go back without…"

"Have you spoken with Monroe? She'll be returning as well."

My lips twitch as the suggestion that Jameson's sister could be a source of companionship. I keep the thought to myself. Despite the fallout from that night's revelations, Monroe had been there. It's true that the Wests stick together.

"Well, you have my number. If you need to chat, I'll be on standby."

For the hourly rate she charges, I almost expect her to come with me and hold my hand tomorrow.

Outside the office, a comforting sight waits for me: Jameson paging through a magazine. When the door opens, he glances up and a blinding smile spreads across his face. His therapy has been going better, judging from how often he gives me that look. "Ready?"

"If you are." I hold out my hand and he takes it.

It's been a little harder for him to let me out of his sight of late. It's one of the issues he's working on with Dr. O'Donnell. Considering that I'm returning for my last year in the morning, I hope they're making progress.

The truth is: being together is the only medicine that seems to work. When he's beside me, I can think about the future without pain. He makes me laugh. At night, we escape in each other's arms for heated, fleeting moments, and when he falls asleep beside me, there are no nightmares.

Despite my objections, our new house has a gate. When I refused to skip out on my last year at Belle Mere, I had to compromise. When we pass, the reporters camped in front of it, it reminds me why he insisted.

"The sale went through," he says, eying me for my reaction.

"Good." I don't think any other response is necessary. When he first told me that he wanted to sell the West Casino, I told him not to bother. Even if a new company slapped another name on it, it would still be there, lingering like a bad memory in the Las Vegas skyline. When he added that the terms of the sale required it to be torn down, I got on board. He's been selling off most of the West real estate holdings ever since.

His phone rings as I grab the milk carton out of the fridge. He checks the screen and sighs.

"Mom or Monroe?" I ask.

"Mom." He accepts the call, wandering into his office.

Getting rid of the casino has freed him up to mediate between his mother and sister. Monroe had surprised all of us when she turned the scandalous leak about her secret identity into a reality show. Jameson took me house shopping the next day.

My own mother had opted to keep her place in Palm Springs, even after I turned down her offer to move in with her. She, along with my dad, had given their blessing for my new living arrangements after some coercion. I'd been forced to flash my diamond ring and ask if they wanted grandbabies now or later. We quickly came to an understanding.

"It's just crass enough to work," Jameson says with disgust as he reappears. "A high school madam. What will reality TV think of next?"

I shudder thinking about it. "She's not going to stop until we're the Kardashians."

"I will never let you be a Kardashian," Jameson promises, earning him a genuine smile.

"That's true love."

"Speaking of love." Jameson swoops down, lifting me off my chair and waiting for my orders.

"Take me to bed," I command.

We linger between the sheets, soaking up our final solitary afternoon before life interrupts our private healing process. This is how we communicate best. Each touch provides a reassurance that we can find nowhere else. We speak to one another in sighs and murmurs with trembling mouths and hungry hands.

When we finally collapse into a heap together, words are still there to fill the space between lovemaking.

"What happens when it's all gone?" I ask in a soft voice.

"What's gone?" he murmurs, nuzzling against my ear.

"The hotels and properties and businesses. What will there be then?"

"You and me," he says simply.

It's not the answer I expect. "That's not much."

"No, it's everything."

The next morning inevitability comes to call. I reluctantly agree to let Jameson drive me to the first day but balk when he offers to pack me a lunch. When we arrive in the parking lot, a few people give us the thumbs up and my throat swells.

"They think I'm a fucking saint." I roll my eyes behind my sunglasses. I'd finally given in and purchased several over-sized pairs.

"Then give them hell, Duchess."

I don't need any encouragement on that end. The board of directors had, in their infinite wisdom, declared that school would start late this year. Extending summer vacation would give students time to mourn and reflect on the tragic events.

You can't make this stuff up.

For most of my peers it just meant impromptu, last-minute vacations.

A car zooms into the spot beside us and honks. Monroe traded in her gold convertible for a Porsche in a shade she deemed "hooker red." I have to hand it to the girl. She has no problem branding herself.

She waits for me to get out, and I sigh. Glancing out the back window, I ask Jameson one more time. "Are you certain Maddox is necessary?"

"Ask me if you want him around when Monroe's film crews show up," he says dryly.

He has a point.

"It's not too late to run."

Jameson's offer is tempting, but I shake my head. "I'm not supposed to run, remember?"

"From me. Running from high school is both understandable and acceptable."

He kisses me long and hard so that my lips are swollen when we break apart. It's a reminder that I'll carry with me throughout the day.

"Finally!" Monroe exclaims, slamming her car door shut. "It's a little creepy that he drops you off."

"You're a call girl," I remind her.

"Touché." She shoulders her bag and prattles on about non-compete clauses and waivers. If nothing else she's taken it as her responsibility to bore me the details of her new show. I interpret it as a sign that she cares.

We both stop short of the entrance.

"This is the last time we'll walk through those doors on a first day." It's uncharacteristically sentimental moment until she adds, "thank God."

But I know she feels the same unwelcoming atmosphere as we enter the building. A sea of unfamiliar faces greets us. Monroe doesn't say it, but I know I'm the closest thing she has to a friend here this year. Even if she had made up with Sabine and Leighton, they'd both transferred to new schools. Jonas had opted to trade places with his sister, going off to school while she came home. And the last I heard, Hugo Roth told the headmaster he was taking a 'leave of absence.'

Monroe bids farewell until later at the door to Advanced Economics. I'm willing to bet she'll teach them a thing or two. Meanwhile, I do my best to ignore the attention I receive as I head toward AP Literature.

Mr. Hunter glances up from the blackboard and I enter.

"Miss Southerly," he says warmly. "I trust you finished your summer reading list."

The normality with which he states this makes my jaw drop open.

"I'm a little behind," I admit.

"Better catch up," he advises, passing out the class syllabus. It's a comfortingly mundane gesture.

At Belle Mère Prep, some kids come back to school after a summer in Europe. Others return with a few new notches on their Restoration Hardware bedposts. So? I'm coming back with a security detail.

They can stare at me in the hallways. Who can blame them? The fact is that I spent most of my summer as a lead suspect in a murder case. My classmates gawk as I take a seat. No doubt they're trying to spot a baby bump. It's the only way this could get any better for them.

Thanks a lot, TMZ.

But while they stare, I can only think of those people that aren't here this morning to start their senior year. I feel their absences as ominously as an unexplained shadow in an empty room. Some are long gone. One didn't see the end of the summer.

Living or dead, they're just ghosts now, and even though they haunt me, I owe it to them to live fully.

ABOUT THE AUTHOR

Geneva Lee is the *New York Times*, *USA Today*, and internationally bestselling author of over twenty novels. Her bestselling Royals Saga has sold nearly two million copies worldwide. She is the co-owner of Away With Words, a destination bookstore in Poulsbo, Washington. When she isn't traveling, she can usually be found writing, reading, or buying another pair of shoes.

Connect with Geneva at:
www.genevalee.com
instagram.com/realgenevalee
facebook.com/genevaleebooks